Stevie Davies was born in Salisbury, Wiltshire, though she lived in Swansea, Wales from a week old, and spent a nomadic childhood in Egypt, Scotland and Germany. After studying at Manchester University, she went on to lecture there, returning to Swansea in 2001. She is Professor of Creative Writing at Swansea University.

Stevie is both a Fellow of the Royal Society of Literature and a Fellow of the Welsh Academy. She has won numerous awards for her fiction, and has been long-listed for the Booker and Orange Prizes. Several of her books have been adapted into radio and screenplays.

She has written for the *Guardian* and *Independent* newspapers, and is a passionate sea-swimmer, cyclist and walker on the Gower. The author of twelve novels, *Equivocator* is her first novella.

EQUIVOCATOR

A Novella

by Stevie Davies

PARTHIAN

Parthian, Cardigan SA43 1ED
www.parthianbooks.com
First published in 2016
ISBN 978-1-910901-47-2
Editor: Robert Harries
Cover design by Robert Harries
Typeset by Elaine Sharples
Printed in EU by Pulsio SARL
Published with the financial support of the Welsh Books Council
British Library Cataloguing in Publication Data
A cataloguing record for this book is available from the British Library.

To the dear memory of
Nigel Jenkins

atque in perpetuum, frater, ave atque vale

1

Have you heard news of my son? Where's he living now?
Perhaps in Orchomenos, perhaps in sandy Pylos
Or off in the Spartan plains with Menelaus?
He's not dead yet, my Prince Orestes, no,
he's somewhere on the earth ...
So we stood there, trading heartsick stories,
deep in grief, as the tears streamed down our faces.

Homer[1]

The face – but more so those expressive hands – unsettles me but I can't look away. There's nothing conventionally attractive about him: in fact he appears rather ruined; his features casually dishevelled. But inviting, like a door ajar. Wherever have I seen this man before? In a fluke of light, as he twists his head, his white hair silvers. I see him doubled, in the reflecting window, a conference celebrity surrounded by yearning networkers. I feel oddly young again, diffident, easily wrong-footed.

Dad flashes into my mind. Not as he was in my childhood but as the litter of bones collected after twenty-nine years in the Zagros Mountains, on the Iranian side of the border with Turkey. Winter by winter fragments of Jack Messenger were reburied in the deep snows of the region; each spring thaw a remnant emerged. And no one saw except the raptors of the mountain that had scattered him. Until last year, when the little that was left of Dad was harvested, identified and brought home.

Wineglasses are handed out at the welcoming table. Mary Jones yoo-hoos me, the renegade palaeontologist from Montana: 'Seb! – Sebastian! Catch you later!' She's been detained by Jarvis Bates of Norwich, world-class bore and expert on cathedrals. The conference, entitled 'What Remains?', has attracted a random crowd of scholars to this shabby Gower college. Little has changed since my earlier visits, except that the gluttonous gulls have made an evolutionary leap, and strut about big as ducks.

Another sidelong glance. The guy – whose name tickles at my memory, not altogether pleasantly – something Spanish? – accepts a glass of red and sips. He seems to listen more than he speaks, though the networkers hang on every word. I palm salted peanuts into my mouth. Escape, I tell myself. An hour and a half until the evening meal.

Slipping away, I cross the main road to the circle of the bay. A sandy slope, dimpled with footsteps, leads down to a plane of level sand. The traffic's roar recedes. In such a gentle space, I think, you can get your bearings. Away from London, breathing salt air, I might find a quieter, less embroiled self to take home to Jesse. Years ago my mother and I would visit the Gower every Easter and summer – and our cottage at Pwll Du seemed far more like home than Fulham ever could.

This morning, as Jesse silently buttered toast, I thought: why are you still feeding me, after last night? He pushed the marmalade towards me and poured tea. When I kissed him goodbye, Jesse flinched. Had he been weeping? How much does he know?

The sea's an opal ellipse, clouded with mist towards the horizon. Across the bay a plume of smoke builds above the steelworks. Someone's digging for cockles; a woman walks a spaniel over the gleaming flats. From the pile driver at the distant pier comes a booming echo. Calm deepens and I ponder walking the Gower coast, skipping this wretched conference: what will I hear anyway but repetitions of repetitions? What would I contribute but regurgitated pap?

However long is it since I've taken time to myself or rather, time off from my selves? You have to give Jesse the truth, I tell myself, you know that. You have – unwillingly, because you do love him, do respect him – deceived him. And he's catching up with you. A tree trunk lies beached: sea-scoured, its body silvered by salt. Seating myself on this beautiful corpse, I look out towards the sea. And breathe.

A figure wends its way from the sea's edge down a zigzag plane of light on water; his, her, reflection travels beneath. The pile driver pulses softly, like the slow heartbeat of some great creature at rest. When I look again, the figure has melted away. No, there he is, seated on another log, with his back to me, gazing out to sea.

As he rises and stretches – a grey-haired man who is not my father – my heart startles and I place the chap. Some Spanish-sounding name – Santana? Santiago? – or Salvator, Salvatore, something like that. And suddenly I'm a wet-behind-the-ears research student at Manchester all those years ago, ogling a glamorous visiting scholar. Now I'm thoroughly unsettled. How did he beat me to the beach? Didn't I catch sight of him as I was dodging out of the welcoming hall, wedged in a corner with poor old Bates? Or was that earlier? He picks his way towards me, trousers rolled up, dangling his shoes by their laces. In the old days the guy was no suit-wearer. He had a look of Che Guevara – at least that's my impression though I doubt if he actually wore the starred beret. I'm sure he didn't.

Seating himself on my log, he starts to dry his feet with a handkerchief. 'I see we had the same idea: far too lovely a day to spend indoors. How are you? We've met, of course,

3

Sebastian. In point of fact we go back a very long way. I've kept up with you. Just read your intriguing monograph on the tomb workers' fragments. I visited Deir el-Medina on the strength of it.'

'Did you really?'

'Oh yes. Your writing style – it brings that dead world to life. Especially the ordinary men and women.'

One can't help but be flattered to have one's baby admired. The artisans who built at the Valley of the Kings left personal letters and bills and records on thousands of ostraca found dumped in a well, fragments that have furnished my obsessive life's work. Ordinary voices speaking to me from deep time. *My* people, they've come to seem. So much remains underground. Wherever you tread in Egypt there's something buried and waiting.

'Well, we've met on the page then, Professor Salvatore,' I reply stiffly. 'I too am aware of your work.'

*

I squirm to recall the callow creature I was in the '80s when he and I crossed paths. I was a nerdy know-all, living in squalor in Rusholme and given to stalking. Could I really have been so creepy? It was Truth I tracked, I told myself, with a capital T. Why Truth should be found amongst mouldy texts in dead languages, I never enquired. Researching for my doctorate in Egyptology, I cruised for anyone showing signs of holding a thread or clue, who might let me tag along. What I loved about my specialism was the way it was fenced around by enigma, deeply encrypted. Snatches of coded conversation waylaid me as I grubbed around in the university library.

'It's all a matter of echo and reflection,' said the earnest

4

student in the lift to his companion. He poked the bridge of his glasses up his nose with his forefinger. It slid down. 'That's how I look at it.'

'Oh so do I,' breathed his obsequious hanger-on. 'Absolutely.'

I'd vaguely noticed them here before. When they headed for the Philosophy stacks, I found myself following. They lingered between K and L. The light had failed in the stack; they groped along the shelves.

'*Mehr Licht!*' chirped the sage student.

'Pardon?'

'More light! Goethe on his death bed, calling for more light.'

The torch beam came from nowhere. As if invoked. It shone straight into the earnest eyes of master and acolyte, who both yelped with shock. The librarian laughed and swept the beam across the rows of books. The lights were forever failing, he said. He'd report it. Yet again. If they came back on this afternoon, Philosophy would be illuminated. Or at least a fragment of it. Darkness might well have fallen on whole continents of knowledge in some other aisle. There would only be one fragment showing at a time – and the rest would have to be guessed.

'It's pesky,' he said. 'But there you are.'

'But this is a university library,' the geek objected. 'Isn't it? We are legitimate readers. It's a travesty.'

'Blame Thatcher, mate, don't blame me. Blame Keith Joseph and the cuts. Nowt to do with me.'

'We'll have to come back later then.'

'Yes, well, you can hardly come back earlier.'

The pair squeezed past me. 'The lights don't work,' they chorused, as if I were deaf. 'Come back later.'

I glimpsed the pair again when the fire alarm sounded and mole-eyed readers were evicted into the glare of day. Bright flocks of shirt-sleeved men and girls in skimpy dresses littered the summer lawns like picnickers. The library's dim vault was my home from home, ghosting around among the friendly dead. With my peers, my mask failed to fit. Nothing would have fitted the shapelessness of me, forever twisting out of true.

Am I substantially different now? Jesse puts my caginess down to my fatherless condition: unfathered or defathered rather, he says. He makes it sound like 'deflowered'. It was when Dad's remains were repatriated that Jesse's unease intensified. Now you've laid him to rest, you can ... surely, Sebs ... move on? Find out who you are and, well, just – be it?

The fire alarm had disturbed my worship of Justin. I'd gleaned his name from some drop-dead gorgeous pal of his who'd bent over whispering, hand on his shoulder. I'd never spoken directly to Justin. Sitting obliquely to him in the reading room, I'd track him with my eyes as he hid Art History text books from other readers, wedging them behind textbooks on probate law. A couple of days before the fire alarm episode, I'd excavated a stash from this mortuary. One volume held a slip of paper. It was how Justin's handwriting would have to be: slant italic, with flamboyant ascenders and descenders. I envied his graceful and old-fashioned arabesques. Perhaps I should take a course on calligraphy.

'See p. 245,' it said. 'Saint Sebastian, the beauteous martyr – tied to a tree and shot full of arrows, ah ha.'

Bloody hell, I thought, and throttled off a laugh. A punctured saint. That'll be me. A virgin with acne scars. Face burning, I leafed through and found the colour plate (bloody hell again) by the painter known as Il Sodoma. The artist apparently swanked about Renaissance Siena and Rome in gaudy gear, trailed by lascivious boys, and kept a menagerie of freakish pets at home. The picture showed a nearly nude androgynous lad draped against a tree, with shoulder-length hair like mine. He'd been deeply penetrated by a trinity of arrows – through neck, ribs and thighs. The tree, with its inevitable allusion to the crucifixion, was also pierced. Above the ecstatic saint's head an angel hovered in a light-burst, offering a crown for Sebastian's tender pains.

Justin must have observed me inspecting his stash. Was this his joke at my expense? I'd bolted, head down.

Now I scanned the crowd milling outside the library. Justin would stand out in any company, a head taller than most, with his sombre face and dark blond hair. The way he held himself reminded me of a washed-out ballet dancer between performances: a louche Nureyev, too languid to launch into the dancer's suspended leaps. He was gay and easy with that. When I spied on Justin, what I searingly suspected about myself – and it killed me, as perhaps something similar had killed my father – became an intuition with which it might be possible to live. But how? I lacked the *élan* to share his world. No graces or style.

Dad had been charismatic, a class act. An adventurer, wayward and charming but – I'd heard my mother say – too needy to be trusted. Whether his travel-writing career was a cover for espionage had never been ascertained and seemed just another tall tale. Jack Messenger's only child had unfortunately turned out a runt. Still, Dad wasn't around to deplore me.

Outside the library someone touched my elbow, lingeringly. 'Excuse me – what's the alarm, do you know?'

'A bomb scare, I heard. Mind you, they're always saying that.'

The enquirer had the look of a professor. If he was not a prof now, he would be. Probably next week. There was something compelling about him. I recognise you, I thought, racking my brains. But where from? It was as if some newscaster had alighted from the television screen, to announce that he'd been watching me.

He gave back my stare, locking into my eyes.

'We've met before,' he said. 'You must remember.'

'I don't think so. Are you on television?'

'Well, I have been. Randomly.'

'Oh.' I didn't like to ask what that was supposed to mean.

The face was arresting, attractive in a craggy way, but wolfish, which I liked. And hungry. He was the kind of man who focuses his entire attention on you. You are the most interesting person in the world, even if he's only asking the time. He looked like an intellectual rebel, unprepared to tolerate the crap the powers-that-be like to ladle out. His voice was pure public school: what we used to call a *hwa-hwa* accent. On the other hand, his dishevelment implied he'd just got up after a night of roiling dreams, hurling on his clothes any old how – cords and an earth-coloured sweater. His abundant hair was all over the place, in a romantic way, I felt, as Byron's might have been.

Did I know a good place for coffee? Or rather, a place for good coffee? When one has travelled in the East, one craves real coffee, he observed. That seemed exotic – and a bit precious. A lecturer in our department had spent a decade in Iran and, hearing that my father was *the* Jack Messenger the Orientalist, invited me regularly to his *soirées* with other sociopathic unfortunates. Dr Arrowsmith seated you cross-legged on Persian rugs and served exquisite glass cups of tea and coffee. Flushed and miserable, you prayed he'd spare you from describing the coffee – its bitter lisp or its burnt almond tang. You prayed there'd be no far-away-eyed reciting of the poets Rumi or Hafez in the original tongue. Oh no, I thought

8

as the stranger asked about coffee, he's one of *those*. Nowadays it's easy to find good coffee: then, there was Real for toffs and Instant for students.

Pitying my awkwardness, the visitor offered his hand. 'Rhys Salvatore. Princeton.' His grey-blue eyes searched into my face as though it interested him deeply. How flattering. 'You are, of course ...'

'Sebastian Messenger. Seb. Researching. Egyptology. But – you don't sound American.'

'Valleys Welshman. From a village you'll not have heard of. Nantymoel.'

I didn't like to mention that he didn't sound like a Welshman either, nor was his surname remotely Welsh.

'Is that where Richard Burton comes from?'

'No. That's Pontrhydyfen.'

'Oh, right. What's your subject?' I asked.

'Ah well, you have me there. I'm a bit of this and a bit of that. A philosophical dabbler. A student of comparative cultures and literatures, notably the Cymric, the Chinese and the Persian. A pirate, really, a traverser of boundaries.'

'Really?' Such postmodern eclecticism was utterly beyond a dumbfounded student of broken pots and hieroglyphs, hunkering in a sandpit with his bucket and spade.

Salvatore smiled. 'Right now I'd settle for halfway decent coffee.'

I pointed out the way to the Senior Common Room and when he invited me to join him, found myself consenting. I doubted whether the professor would find many intellectuals to converse with there. The SCR, haunted by emeritus dons nodding off over journals, was one step away from a nursing home.

As we advanced together over the quad, the visitor's fame and charisma acted as a magnet. Youngish lecturers swivelled

9

in mid-stride and headed across the concourse, gliding in his wake, stray ducklings cleaving to a long-lost mother duck. When I tried to slip away, Salvatore started introducing me: 'I don't know if you've met Sebastian Messenger. He is an up-and-coming Egyptologist, researching into … I'm sorry, Sebastian, I didn't quite catch?'

Scarlet, I mumbled something about the Egyptian Book of the Dead. And that I'd just remembered I had an appointment. To discuss it. The Book, that is. Of the Dead.

The guy appeared oddly reluctant to let me go – and fond, like an uncle. He'd catch up with me, he said, and we'd talk properly. We knew each other, he repeated. From way back.

I felt, as I loped back to the library, that I had obscurely disappointed the stranger, starving him of some nourishment he craved. And that, if I turned my head, I'd see him gazing after me.

'Oy, watch where you're fucking going, wanker.'

'Sorry.' I realised I was running in an arc, dreamily skewed. I slowed down to a walk.

That afternoon there occurred a luminous interlude in the stacks. All the lights were functioning but the two earnest young truth-seekers weren't around to luxuriate in it. I ran my eyes over venerable volumes under K-L and wondered what the self-appointed sage had been looking for. Kant? Kierkegaard? Lacan? Lavater? Or perhaps, nothing in particular. Perhaps it was all show. He might have been a hollow vessel with a yen for disciples. Or an ambitious competitor spreading disinformation.

Go to S, I told myself. Find Rhys Salvatore. But Salvatore's *oeuvre* was incomprehensible. It flitted between languages with mandarin aplomb. It was on the trail of a cosmic *aporia*, so the blurbs indicated. But what might an *aporia* be, when it was at home? Apparently it had no home. An impasse, a state

of puzzlement, a point of doubt and indecision, a kind of hole, explained a dictionary, where meaning deconstructs itself.

Right. A hole. And this geezer is actually hunting for this insoluble impasse, I thought? The heroic search for a drain or sump? And he is paid for this?

I headed towards Travel. Although I owned a copy of everything he wrote, and avoided reading them, I still found myself heading to the shelves in case another imprint might present a different face. All Dad's books were out.

*

'I've been hoping to catch up with you.' Salvatore seems ageless, though he must be bordering on elderly. At the same time he doesn't appear terribly healthy. As if he didn't sleep. 'You are rather elusive, you know, Sebastian. Whenever I land, you take off.'

This is so like what Jesse said last night – 'You're never *here*, Seb – even when you *are* here' – that I can hardly breathe. I'm with Jesse under false pretences, is my partner's theme. He *knows*: 'I followed you,' he blurted. 'On one of your night-walks.'

'I've several times attended conferences,' Salvatore continues. 'For instance, the Cairo conference last year – where I missed you by a whisker! My daughter was with me. It would have been nice to introduce you. Anyway, we had a good conference and afterwards we stayed on a few days at Luxor, a haunt of yours. But I knew you and I would catch up with each other again. How are you?'

'Fine, yes – thanks.'

'Yes, but *really*. How are you?'

If you wanted to get in touch, I think, there's always the internet. There are so many ways of tracing people.

11

Altogether too many. Nobody can hide these days. There's a sense of *déjà vu*. You have been peering out of the shadows, I think, and shiver: and somehow with Dad's eyes. Melting eyes, variable between blue and grey. Why am I thinking that? Ludicrous. I ought to ask point blank. But, if I ask, he might tell me.

The tide: it's advancing too swiftly. It waits until we're not looking and makes a dash forwards.

And now Salvatore – as he was always going to do – speaks Dad's name.

Jack Messenger, he says. He knew Jack. As schoolboys. And later, of course. Your father, he says, was a genius. And I was so sad when. Of course it was the loss to you and your. Yes. Oh, I can't speak about it, forgive me. We lost touch, Salvatore mourns in a curious piping wail. And then when they brought back his. His remains. From Turkey. Did they ever find out how he?

'No,' I say, to cut him off, and start to rise. He doesn't touch me but I feel detained, and sink back down.

'Jack was the only genius I ever knew.'

Aside from yourself, I don't say.

And then Salvatore raises the topic of the shed. The shed, he is saying, when they dug it up. Your father's writing shed in the garden? The shed. The den. Not the shed itself of course, but what they found underneath.

Perhaps it was my nightmares that have always convinced me that I saw the cadaver they unearthed. Right down to the smell that over the years has assailed me from time to time, passing a restaurant ventilator shaft or lugging rubbish out to the bin. I couldn't possibly have seen the corpse. My mother and I had been evicted for the police search and stayed away for weeks. The body was not Dad's. I never thought it was.

'Everybody assumed …,' he says.

'Yes, but it wasn't.'

'No, of course not. And then. Last year. He was found and brought home. A kind of closure for you and your family.'

Closure? What is this closure they all talk about?

Salvatore wonders, by the way, whether Dad left a Persian manuscript or any letters from his last visit to Iran? He assumes not. Salvatore has been in touch with Jack's publisher but the lady who used to edit him is either dead or has moved on (can't people tell the difference?) and nobody appears to know anything.

No, I say, there's nothing. And if there were, wouldn't it have been published? I think: the old guy's just a nosy-parker with perfectly false teeth perched on a log pulling on his socks.

'We were at school together – he was *the* friend of my youth, Sebastian. And I have access to papers of his – I'll be happy to share – I want you to meet my daughter – '

I consult my watch. The sea has sidled nearer. Waves are tonguing in, making progress with every surge. How they covered all that ground is a mystery, unless we've been here far longer than I'm aware. Without answering, I excuse myself and, turning away, retrace my steps across the sand.

'Don't run off, Sebastian,' he calls, as if I were a child escaping from leading reins, and he hurries behind me, panting, apologising for touching a nerve, if he has, he's terribly sorry: what is my talk about this evening?

'The Abomination of Monthu!' I call, without slackening pace, and even to me this sounds thoroughly inane and my behaviour appears infantile. And I think: I'll go home to Jesse now, and offer him some clarity. I'll ask him please to forgive my follies, which is all they are, and to stay, for he's all the world to me. I'll say: it's not so much falsehoods we live with

13

as the habit of silence. Let me bring truth out into the open between us. And I know I won't, because I'm shot through with all these voluptuous arrows and tied to a tree.

*

Manchester, 1986. It was, I think, the following day when I again spotted the Spanish Welshman from Princeton, in the library foyer where they exhibited a sixteenth century printing press. The machine resembled a mediaeval torture instrument, I always thought: a dual purpose thumb-screw and rack. Salvatore stood with folded arms, a scuffed briefcase at his feet. Dad had owned one like it, bought in Germany. He'd been hiking in the Schwarzwald searching out old Nazis to interview. Not finding any, he'd made some up off the top of his head, so I overheard him drunkenly boasting to some pal – and they both cracked up laughing. That book – that fiction – had sold well and it kept on selling, even or especially when its methodology and conclusions came into question.

I sought the briefcase after he'd disappeared. I was thirteen. At first I accepted – and my mother bitterly believed, for reasons she never precisely disclosed – that Jack had deserted us. Without a word. Jack liked people to think he was working for the Soviets, she said, or the Shah, or the Bolivians; makes out he's Philby and Maclean all rolled into one. And perhaps he was, how do I know? I'm changing my name, she said. Her eyes were half closed with weeping. (Don't, I said, don't change your name – it's my name too). My mother sobbed, I heard her, into her pillow in the night. I sobbed too. There were no sightings. Dad's bank account remained untouched.

Jack Messenger had hung out in some of the world's most

14

iffy places. He'd become persona non grata in most of them. He gravitated towards turmoil and conflict, especially the kind of conflict that's volatile, where spurious alliances twist and turn on one another. Jack haunted murderous frontiers and acquainted himself with gangsters, drug-pushers, people-smugglers. I understood none of that at the time. But I sensed the high-voltage excitement of Dad, waves of electricity streaming off his skin. I felt his charm when he flashed the searchlight of his attention on me. Dad was the one whose bedtime stories I hankered after, despite the fact that they kept me awake and seeded themselves in my imagination as lifelong nightmares.

Books remained, and his second pair of specs, an Olivetti Lettera typewriter, but not the briefcase. It was intimately Dad. As a kid I'd enjoyed rooting around in its secret pockets. It had accompanied Jack wherever he went.

He left eleven major works, the most famous being *Swimming across the Desert* as well as a big book on post-colonial Africa, *Sunset, Sunrise*. They are darkly witty, ironic, anecdotal – poised between devil-may care and diffidence. Jack presents himself as an innocent abroad, in a state of permanent surprise as he barges into one revealing mishap after another. Chameleon Jack invents himself differently wherever he finds himself, and never as the father of this son. A sorrowing son who would once upon a time have followed him to the ends of the earth. It was years since I'd looked into Dad's writings. The last time I'd dipped in, the book seemed to exhale at me with scalding breath. It hurt to read his suavely jaunty words about terrifying things – fratricide, massacres, trauma. I kept the books. I kept them closed.

He wasn't in the books anyway. A real self (if there was one) hunkered behind the Jack Messenger persona. Returning with his traveller's tales, Dad would study my response and I began to appear in humorous preludes and codas. Well, a version of me. I featured as Kernel, the lad next door over the narrator's fence, with scarred knees and a missing front tooth, given to uttering unintended ironies that cut the heroic wayfarer down to size.

Larger than life despite his small stature, Jack was the teller of tales, dancer of dances. He'd visited the Sufi whirlers of Turkey and spun in our sitting-room wearing a flared skirt of my mother's, rotating on the ball of one foot, faster and faster, like the wheeling planets, he said. He'd pick me up and spin me with him, till I was almost sick with a rapture of giddy giggling. – *This is how the cosmos turns and now we are the cosmos, we – Jack and Sebastian Messenger – are the planets and the space between, we are all that is! Can't you feel it?* This would end in his tossing me up and catching me three times, 'in a holy fashion'. He'd studied judo in Japan, the way of gentleness, the soft way, he'd say, upending me with one hand and showing me the trick of throwing him.

At other times my father was remote, rancid. He sucked at the bottle into the early hours; next day we'd tiptoe round him. He might not get up till late afternoon: *leave me fucking alone for fucksake.* He'd lumber into his shed and reappear with a growth of stubble, snarling. He'd vanish altogether for weeks at a time. My parents were more often apart than together. And who was Jack when Dad wasn't with us?

Don't be like your father, Seb. Don't.

I understand – and did, imperfectly, at the time – that my mother had no intention of blackening Dad's name to me. Her plea burst out when her heart broke and afterwards I saw her, intelligent and just woman as she was – is, despite the frailty of age – attempting to rescind or soften what she'd said. But once the acid has spurted on your face, you're condemned to wear the scar and confirm it daily in the mirror.

I was free of them both, I told myself once I escaped to Manchester. Now for my own life.

But Rhys Salvatore unleashed dark memories and presentiments. Here he was in the library foyer. He turned to the lift, without acknowledging me. Trailing him to the Rare Books and Manuscripts Room, I watched through the blinds as he settled his briefcase on the chair beside him and pulled on the obligatory white gloves to handle the documents. As he worked, he seemed to be grinning to himself. I think at this point I must have taken myself off to the reading room. That day turned out to be one of the most important of my life, or so I thought for the next few weeks and months and years, because of what happened with Justin Knight, taking the pair of us to the refectory for lunch and afterwards up to his mysterious room in the Tower.

I was so flabbergasted when Justin sat down next to me, draping his arm across my chair-back, that I could hardly reply.

'Sebastian, aren't you? Wow, Egyptology! That is cool. Mummies and so on! I adore mummies.'

Mummies do have allure. In point of fact I've never been particularly fascinated with Pharaohs' processed cadavers. Their relentless carnality leaves me cold. It's the ordinary folk that hold me bound – the artisans who dug and decorated the tombs. But I chatted to Justin about mummification as if it constituted the passionate centre of my intellectual life. I offered him a guided tour of the Egypt Centre. And Dr Rosalie David was unwrapping a mummy this very week. Would he like to observe?

'Cool,' he said. 'But what about a bite to eat on the way?'

The day began to whirl. It all happened so quickly, too quickly. That morning I was a virgin, hatefully a virgin, shamefully a virgin, and by late afternoon I had been (as I put it to myself) loved by a man.

17

I am loved, I thought, I'm loved, Justin loves me, he loves me.

That was my mistake, of course: Justin was wiling away an afternoon in the nicest way he knew, which involved giving as well as taking pleasure. Later I stood on Oxford Road and observed the flow of traffic, while tides of students broke and reformed around me. Life had opened its arms to Seb Messenger. He'd never be the same. I wanted to laugh and cry but did neither: just stood and observed the workmen, perched high on scaffolding, sand-blasting generations of soot off the Whitworth Hall and the Egypt Centre, revealing surfaces of pale, sunlit stone.

Don't spoil it for yourself, warned an inner voice. *Don't put pressure. Give him space. You have no call on Justin. Be satisfied.*

Be satisfied with hunger?

You know what the wise course of action is, of course you do, but your feet direct you otherwise. My whole existence up to that afternoon felt drearily unlived. I lurked in the library, in case Justin returned. Maybe he'd be at a loose end and we could go for a drink or make that deferred tour of the mummies. Just as I was getting to my feet, there was a sizzling sound like rashers in a pan and all the lights went out. The library lay in twilight.

'I'm not standing for this,' muttered the Geek to himself. I hadn't noticed him there, cruising the stacks alone, minus his parasite. 'I'm just not. It's beyond a joke.'

What the hell was he playing at? He held a cigarette lighter up to the book titles, squinting. The cap clicked, the lighter sparked and there was a hiss. The flame held steady and then, as if a draught had found it, it leaned sideways and there was a stink of singed leather.

'Oh shit. No!' He snapped the lighter off and scarpered. Alarms rang. The library began to evacuate again. Following

18

the crowd, I made up my mind to let Justin take the next step in our affair (if it was an affair). *Don't look pathetic. You are pathetic but he doesn't know that (probably) and you don't have to advertise it.*

As I approached the exit, I thought my way around the wonders of Justin's study bedroom: an emerald satin counterpane (or silk, was it?); a trio of African heads in polished wood, a carriage clock and an acoustic guitar.

Was this Taste? Or was his room basically a bit of a junk shop? I brooded upon it all. How could I possibly invite this sophisticate round to my squalid pit, the two-roomed flat in Platt Lane, rich in nothing but my father's books? Last night I'd encountered in my kitchen a cockroach in a crusted spillage of sugar. The insect crouched under the bilious light as if it owned the place. And there was I, bent over it, not in the least disgusted by my tenant, thinking of the god Khepri, associated with the scarab or dung beetle – and how the dung beetle's antennae seemed to clasp the dung ball, rolling it over the sand, like the solar disc flanked by a pair of horns. The Egyptians had believed that the scarabs' young emerged spontaneously from dung balls, self-generated. Khepri was key to rebirth and resurrection.

I'd actually carted a chair into the kitchen and sat down to study this verminous visitor. A kind of Egyptian field-trip in deepest Rusholme. The insect's forequarters were furiously busy. Fetching a magnifying glass, I observed the cockroach grasping the base of an antenna with its spiny little feet and threading this through its mouthparts. It was grooming so as to be able to sniff out the sugar-coated world festering around it, provided by myself for its family and friends.

I'd have to clean, perhaps even fumigate, before I could invite my lover round. In the end, I'd flicked the roach off with my fingernail and it scuttled for cover in the wainscot.

Too late, pal: I crunched it under my sole. Who knew what smashed cadavers lay on the mortuary world of my linoleum? Not that I never mopped that floor – but the soapy water did not, I suspected, penetrate far beneath the surface muck.

Despite the fire alarm, I lingered in the library. It was a way of pegging myself down. But then it happened.

The flash and crash, a billowing of smoke, scared the crap out of me and I took to my heels. Outside amongst swirling crowds, a weird sense of repetition took over. For here, precisely where he'd stood at the time of the first exodus, was the visiting professor. Everything reels round; everything repeats itself, I thought, and gave a little jerk as you do when waking from the verge of sleep. In the afternoon's excitements, I'd forgotten the guy. Salvatore had not forgotten me. He greeted me like an old friend, with the same look in his eyes – melting, endeared. 'My dear Seb,' he said, and reached out to touch my hand. Every nerve was still alive from Justin's love-making: Salvatore's touch seemed to scald my skin.

Was I all right? Was it an IRA bomb this time, he wondered? It wasn't so very long since the Brighton Bombing and the attempted assassination of the Thatcher cabinet. I shook my head but said no more. For some reason I was going to keep the Geek's secret. I gaped at the scuffmarks on the professor's briefcase. It was bulging – fuller than when he'd gone in.

Every alarm in the city was going off. People were running. Fire engines and ambulances. Police. Cordons. Lights were set up in the quad, trained on the library, bright as those in a football ground.

I thought, in my melodramatic way, of the Royal Library of Alexandria going up in flames: it had held a copy of every book in the world, or so they boasted. A hundred scholars resided there full-time, teaching and studying. The world's intellectual heart pulsed in the city – a kind of university, with gardens and eateries. Whereupon along comes some lunatic Geek and torches half a million unique works. All incinerated in a moment. Can be done.

'Well,' said Salvatore. 'I'm glad you're unhurt, Sebastian. Let me buy you a meal. Look here, I want to come clean. About your father.'

'Yes, and – excuse me – but – surely – your briefcase – '.

He clutched it to him with both arms. Like a dead baby.

'That's his,' I broke out. 'It is. I know it is. What are you doing with it? Look – this mark. I made it. With a pin. Dad was furious when I did that. I sketched mountaineers planting a flag. Look. Here. See? I whined, *The pin did it, Dad, not me, it was the pin!* – And that made Dad laugh and he wasn't cross any more. Where did you get it, Dr Salvatore? And – I'm sorry but – but why are you – ?'

A fleet of cabs was parked in the nearby cul-de-sac. And now it was my turn to pursue the visitor. 'Oh dear no,' he said, quite coldly, and hugged the briefcase to his chest. 'You are mistaken. Must fly.'

2

I am at no loss for information about you and your family;
but I am at a loss where to begin. Shall I relate how your
father Tromes was a slave in the house of Elpias, who kept
an elementary school near the Temple of Theseus, and how
he wore shackles on his legs and a timber collar round his
neck? Or how your mother practised daylight nuptials in
an outhouse next door to Heros the bone-setter, and so
brought you up to act in tableaux vivants and to excel in
minor parts on the stage?

Demosthenes[2]

In those days, I remind myself, I was intense and callow. If
anyone wanted an *aporia,* I was a perfect example. Doubtless
my memory of that first meeting is coloured out of all
recognition. Had Salvatore really filched something from the
library as I suspected and run off with it in a briefcase taken
from my father? Surely not.

'Rhys Salvatore,' I say casually to Jarvis Bates of Norwich.
'What do you know about him?'

We're both up early, fuelling ourselves for conference
tedium. Jarvis tucks into a fry-up as if he hadn't eaten for a
week: the congealing grease scarcely looks appetising.

'Well, only what people say.'

'Which is?'

'Salvatore's a riddle wrapped in an enigma. Or at least
that's what he likes you to think. Big reputation, mind,
amongst postmodernists. He's a magpie, spouts the lingo.

And since Derrida died, he's the one remaining oracle aboveground.' Jarvis mops up the greasy yolk with a hank of bread and lolls back, sighing and patting his paunch as if to sympathise with its bursting plight. 'You know, Seb, I really shouldn't,' he pleads. 'But the grub is there, isn't it? It needs hoovering up. Somebody's got to do it.' Jarvis looks pasty and tired. I think: you're my age, but look at you.

Off Jarvis waddles to fetch toast. Returning, he adds that no two witnesses see the same man. Salvatore's a charmer all right, and a subtle, devious guy: in a kind of meaningless Cymric way. Since we're enjoying Welsh hospitality, the foghorning of this sentiment seems less than tactful. I flush, ashamed for Bates, who isn't remotely bothered.

'Well now, I was guesting at an Oxford college,' he goes on. 'The gentry breakfasts at High Table are out of this world. Kedgeree! Who eats kedgeree nowadays? I sampled a bit of everything, just to show willing. Anyway, Salvatore had recently visited. The Fellows were praising his exquisite mind. As it turned out, nobody could reconstruct what Salvatore had been arguing for or against. I mean, who even knows what his subject is? The Terracotta Army? King Arthur? Sheherezade? Salvatore's a Farsi speaker and nobody at the Oxford talk was: that was probably it. He blinded them with his own brand of postcolonialism.'

'Really, he speaks Farsi?' I think of Dad's Iranian passion and how he adored the language and said: If you knew Farsi, Kernel, you wouldn't want to speak English, Farsi is the most sensual, spiritual of tongues.

'Yes,' says Jarvis. 'Rhys spent some time in Iran – BA – Before Ayatollah – and had a lucky escape apparently, come the Revolution. And then he suffered some kind of breakdown, went off the map for a while, fingers bright ginger from smoking. Likewise teeth. He must have got a new set of gnashers in the States. He doesn't talk about any of that. He has a daughter apparently – he dotes on her – but I've never heard of a wife.'

I dawdle over the international pages of the newspaper when Bates has gone to inspect his notes: he's chairing all day, 'for his sins'.

The situation in Iran looks modestly hopeful: President Rouhani is extending an olive branch to the West, heretofore 'The Great Satan'. *Nobody who visits Iran ever really comes back home*, I remember my father saying: I was a child and it stuck in mind because I thought it odd, given that he had come home. But then of course he didn't. And Salvatore did. At about the same epoch.

When I look up, Salvatore is in the breakfast queue, chatting with Mary Jones, that other anomaly, who, to the not quite universal disdain of her peers, claims to have teased surviving biological material out of dinosaur fossils sixty-five million years old. My attention snags on his briefcase. Salvatore cuddles it as he chats, as if he can feel it purr. Outside seabirds keen between the buildings, a desolation of gulls.

I fold the newspaper, with the idea of returning to my room, skipping the morning's presentations. I'll ring Jesse and leave immediately after my own paper, or at least first thing tomorrow. I begin to text: I miss you so badly, let's talk, really talk when I —

But no. The guy materialises with his tray. 'Now, don't rush off, Seb. Coffee? I hope that's how you like it?'

Salvatore unloads his breakfast – croissants and several miniature pots of honey, for he's telling me he has a sweet tooth and can't get through a morning without a sugar hit.

'Chatting to your good friend, Mary Jones,' he says. 'My fellow Welshwoman, so she claims. Ten generations back!

She's travelling west, to Fishguard and Haverfordwest, to trace her ancestors. Firstly, their memorials and monuments – in remote churchyards on the western edge of Wales. Then she plans to scout amongst the Joneses of Pembrokeshire for branches of her family that might share her DNA. What she's done for dinosaurs she plans to do for Joneses! Told her there are a tidy lot of Joneses in Wales. She grinned and said: yeah, I know, Rhys, but the magic is in the quest. I can't disagree with that.'

Pleased with the southern drawl he's produced to mimic Mary, Salvatore lodges the briefcase beside him and settles his jacket over the chair-back. 'Let me remind you,' he says, breaking open a croissant, 'of where and when we first met.'

'Manchester. 1986,' I come in. 'There was a fire in the library. And it turned out that valuable manuscripts had gone missing from the Rare Books Department.'

'If memory serves, they thought it was an IRA bomb,' Salvatore says in a measured way. 'But I wasn't meaning that. I knew you long before, Sebastian.'

I shake my head.

'I'm not saying that you can be expected to remember me. Oh dear. Are you quite yourself, Sebastian? Nothing wrong, is there?'

Dad peers at me out of Rhys's eyes. The voice seems to travel back across continents. Salvatore comes apart into flocks of whirling dots. Dread overwhelms me. Hang on, I tell myself: migraine aura, that's all.

Was there ever a time when Salvatore wasn't looming? Deep in my childhood, yes, you were there.

At the next table they're discussing, with reference to Bishop Berkeley and Ludwig Wittgenstein, whether Tony Blair is a real person. Explosions of mirth.

'Bit of a headache coming on.'

Through the generalised hubbub, I overhear Salvatore breathing. Very loud, it seems. What's the word? Stertorous. Getting worse. It's offensive, the way he breathes. Intimate acts should remain just that, intimate acts. Keep yourself to yourself, I think. My distaste mounts, for now he's introducing a morsel of honeyed bread into his moist mouth and I hear Salvatore swallow. He chafes his fingertips fussily to rid them of flakes of croissant. I hear that too, magnified. Then he goes on masticating. More and more invasively. Can he not control this obscene breathing, this in-your-face fuck-you breathing: I have to run or do him violence. I manage neither, fists wedged in my jacket pockets.

It's that bloody thing you used to get in your teens, I tell myself. Adolescent disgust wrought to a pitch of morbid intensity. Misophonia: the technical diagnosis St Thomas's Hospital revealed to my mother. At least there was a name for her son's weirdness. It will pass, said the consultant, with adolescence. Probably.

Salvatore's nails scrape across the table-top as he rises to fetch more 'reviving coffee'. Just go, I think, piss off. Go and breathe on someone else. He has left behind his jacket and briefcase.

As I quit the refectory with long strides, my father's briefcase under my arm, the blood-boiling rage subsides. There's something badly wrong with me, I think. I need help, I have always needed it. The feeling I have is murderous. Turning round at the door, I see Salvatore approach our table with the coffee, pausing to pass the time of day with Jarvis Bates – and I recognise afresh Jack Messenger peering from his face.

*

The first evening lecture, by Professor Jones of Montana, is controversial. Last year Mary published her sensational discovery of microscopic quantities of living tissue surviving in dinosaur bones. That should, of course, be impossible, for bones turn literally to stone over the millennia, absorbing the minerals in the surrounding rock. Orthodoxy holds that the marrow would all have decayed and disappeared, millions of years ago. Her findings will radically change palaeontology, Mary insists, when her colleagues update their Victorian mentalities.

Question-time swells into uproar. Mary's expression is beatific: let asses bray, it's what they do! The Chair calls for order. After all this drama, my post-migraine remarks on Monthu will appear a specious footnote to centuries of academic nitpicking. The dinosaurs are the real thing.

I hardly care. I've got the briefcase, whose compartments I scoured until my fingers found the memory stick. In my pocket, it feels hot. Here is a find, disinterred from a deep stratum, potentially holding cryptic living tissue. But what am I looking for and how will it satisfy me to track that anachronistic stranger, my father? Yes, it will matter. I'll have to halt my endless digressions and look into the face of truth, taking stock and considering the future. For Jesse and myself.

I introduce the topic of the ostraca. Mary, in the front row, exhibits a repertoire of nervous tics, repressed during her talk. I praise her revolutionary work, adding that my own find might be thought modestly analogous to cellular tissue in ancient rock – well, clay, in this case. The ostraca have everything to tell us about the builders of the Pharaohs' tombs.

The letter I read aloud is from an unknown woman to a man whose wife she accuses of adultery: 'Your wife's crime,' she spits, 'is the Abomination of Monthu! I will make you recognise this continuous fornication which your wife has committed against you.'

Jarvis Bates, in the Chair, rests folded arms on his paunch and ruminates; his eyelids droop and he slumbers. The lecture theatre is less than half full, conferrers having sloped off to the bar after the ritual stoning of Mary. She plucks at her pink cardigan, as if removing one by one the goads slung at her in the course of the evening. Rhys Salvatore sits forward intently, chin on hands. Perhaps he ponders the whereabouts of his briefcase.

Although in point of fact, he all but offered it to me. A mnemonic and a lure.

How long have I paused? The memory stick is a chip of ice. Rhys Salvatore's face, I see, resembles that of a mourner. His expression is harrowing. His eyes grasp at mine and pull, hard. Looking down at my notes, I break his hold.

Monthu, I explain, was a mighty god whose name appears on Egyptian marriage certificates. A force to be reckoned with. Who'd want to tangle with a Power originating in the murderous heat of the sun? One glance from Monthu might fry you to a crisp. Was the falcon-headed war god perhaps himself deceived by one of his three divine spouses? It is in the nature of men and gods to betray and be betrayed, I reflect. The face of Rhys Salvatore, the mourner in the black suit, twists with pain. But in general the expressions on the faces of those who might loosely be called my listeners advise, 'Wake us up when you've something to say that means anything. Anything at all.'

I take a few desultory questions. Someone explodes in spasms of sneezing and seems fated to keep it up to eternity. Weariness engulfs me: all this self-important blather I've devoted my life to. About beings who not only don't exist but never have. Figments. Fragments of figments.

And then it's time to lead my party into the bowels of Egypt. In the college's little Egypt Centre, the Room of the

Dead is dim, precisely as it should be, for light licks the lustre off ancient paint. Each issued with a wind-up torch, we squint through glass at mummified shrews and kittens. There are rows of shabti figures, doll-like clay models representing the servants on whom the dead must depend in the Underworld: the Field of Reeds will require tilling and sowing and reaping. Each lazy dead person needed 401 labourers to complete a year's work on his behalf, so these little guys are legion. The mummiform figures, equipped with hoes and mattocks and sacks, look tired out already. They are mud men, not faience, and fashioned for use not ornament.

On a wall is a diagram of the Pyramid of the Pharaoh Unis in Saqqara, featuring the burial chamber and the room containing Unis's Ka-statue, the perfect double of the Pharaoh. When you died, I explain, your soul split into two, the Ba departing every morning to keep an eye on your family, the Ka swanning off to the Land of Two Fields, to enjoy the luxury fruits of the shabtis' labours. Every night Ka and Ba popped home for a night's kip in the mummy. But what if your mummy had been raided or your Name erased? The Ba and Ka would be cut off. There was no way home. You would lose yourself forever.

The conference members are fascinated. I recite to them the infamous Cannibal Hymn inscribed on the antechamber to Pharaoh Unis's tomb.

The sky rains down.
The stars darken.
The celestial vaults stagger.
The bones of Aker tremble.
The stars are stilled against them,
at seeing Pharaoh rise as a Ba.
A god who lives on his fathers and feeds on his mothers.

Four thousand years back, Unis had been an unusually big eater. How to gain access to the power of the gods? Devour them! What else? Pharaoh's mummy consumes one-by-one every god it meets. Only a handful of gods elude Unis's cooking-pots, these being the divine cooks and bottle-washers. Otherwise down Pharaoh's gullet they go: big gods for lunch, medium gods for dinner and tiddlers for a little light supper. The engorged Unis, I tell them, is a fantasy of omnipotence. And in the end, what is he? Still hungry.

*

At dinner Mary and I match one another glass for glass. She describes the Hell Creek Formation in the badlands of Montana, sketching a map on the back of the menu, in case I visit and feel like digging up a dinosaur.

'Plenty of fossils to go round, Seb. Millions, literally. We make a useful little income for the Centre by charging amateur diggers. Everyone adores a dinosaur, after all.'

'One day they'll all be gone.'

'Yeah. But by then humankind will have given way to the insects.'

Rhys Salvatore, penned at a corner table amongst admirers, glances across with an expression of helpless yearning. He's mouthing something: 'See you afterwards?'

Mary and I continue drinking through the speechifying. The main course, announces the head waiter, will shortly be served. There are some quite minor hitches in the kitchens. Salvatore waves; he beckons. He rises in his seat. Come, he seems to say, I want you, I need you. And I almost get up, I almost go.

'Rhys is ogling you,' Mary says. 'Don't look. Unless you fancy him, of course. Sorry. Just joking.'

'Seriously though, Mary – what do you make of him?'

'A friend of mine taught with him at Princeton. Brilliant, he said, charming, but a bit of a hyena – always loping after other people's kills, was how Ben put it. He noticed that Salvatore's a mimic. *He do the Police in different voices!* Watch out for when he's least Valleys and most Dylan Thomas. And light-fingered, my friend said: no grasp of the difference between *meum* and *tuum*. But another friend said that was all surface. She said that when she heard her husband had died, Rhys happened to be with her. He held her – and cried with her. He stayed with her all night, just holding her. He fed her with a teaspoon when she couldn't eat. Said he had been there and knew her grief. So take your pick really. Why?'

'Oh, nothing. Idle curiosity.'

At last the main course arrives: risotto that's been left out in the rain. Before we've finished, waiters are removing dishes and side-plates. They do so with baleful courtesy: they'll not be sorry to see the back of us. One seems to have taken root directly behind me. If I turn my head slightly, I can make out his dark shape.

Then he places one hand on my shoulder. His other hand comes down on the other shoulder. He gives the gentlest of gentle pushes.

I swing round. Nobody there. Bloody hell. Too much bad plonk. And bad it is. Why do I never learn? Among the bits and shreds in my pocket, the memory stick seems to buzz. Or was that my mobile? Bed, I think. Then home. But Mary is still puzzling away at Salvatore.

'In the end,' she says, 'isn't he just another sad case? – I mean, look at him now. Does he look well? Even though he's surrounded by avid disciples, does he look happy? You know what Plato says? – love is lack. Rhys is starved and nothing he swallows sustains him.'

'And me?'

'You've got a bit more going for you, Seb dear. The guy's probably after your ostraca. Wants to relate them to his potty theories of Camelot and – I don't know – Viking chessmen. God, these conferences,' she says and yawns extravagantly. Mary doesn't mind who hears and her voice is carrying. Heads swivel; her serial yawns start others off. The yawns go round and the paroxysmic speaker at the top table passes his hand over his gaping mouth and drones on.

'Why do we do it, Seb? Tell me that! Your face feels like rubber at the end of any conference. Your mind has gone, you're moronic for weeks, it comes over you to drown yourself in a handy lake. What's that? A memory stick? You want to open it?'

She plugs it into her tablet. '*Your Father Wore a Wooden Collar,* by Rhys Iwan Salvatore. Catchy title! *After Thucydides.* Good grief, four hundred pages of bullshit.'

She scrolls through an immense document freighted with half-page footnotes – and the footnotes have spawned footnotes of their own. There are endnotes to the secondary footnotes. '*The question of the self: who am I not in the sense of who am I but rather who is this I that can say who? What is the I and what becomes of responsibility once the identity of the I trembles in secret?* Oh boy,' she says and hoots. 'I am so trembling in secret here, Seb! Hey, what about this: *I do not teach truth as such; I do not transform myself into a diaphanous mouthpiece of eternal pedagogy.* Yeah, that's me, diaphanous, goggling. A whole chapter to the *aporia*. Do I really want to know what that is? But you're going to tell me, Seb, I can see that. Do so in no more than three words.'

'It's a hole,' I say.

'Right. Shall we drink up and sidle off?'

32

*

The room bucks, a deck in a swell. Now it slowly sinks, for we're the men who went to sea in a sieve, in spite of all their friends could say. Am I about to throw up? Swallow some water. Glad Jesse isn't here to see me pissed.

I find myself in the power-shower. Fuck me if I know how I got here but the hot water is tonic as it hammers the nape of my neck. It possesses thumbs and the thumbs understand the art of massaging deep into your muscles and kneading your scalp in a frankly voluptuous way. How many guys have wanked under this state-of-the-art shower? The pipes bang. No, it's the door. Fuck off, it's one in the morning. Or even two. I slick back my hair, shambling from the bathroom with a towel round my waist.

The rapping again. Jesus Christ, I can hear breathing. Through the door. Is it the old guy with a wooden collar round his neck?

If I lie down, there's a distinct danger of throwing up. Tea might help? En route to the kettle, I seem to have detoured in a surprising arc, to find myself at the door. I squint through the peephole.

There he stands, head bent in an attitude of thoughtful waiting. Panic: I step back. It's alright: he can't see you. (Can he?) I plump down on the end of the bed, which tilts.

I should just go and punch the bugger's lights out. Obvious answer. A real man would do just that. But I'm not. A real man. Am I? What is a real man? Big conundrum. A bit like logarithms. What is a logarithm, I asked Sir. Where is it? What does it look like? It is not a solid body, Sir informed the mathematical dunce. You won't find one under your bed, Messenger. There was a braying of classroom mirth.

Don't be like your father, Seb, she said: don't. He's such a

33

liar, she said. He believes his own narcissistic fantasy of himself. Or was that Salvatore? One of the two and which is which?

Was Jack a real man or not a real man? There's no knowing.

Has my ancient stalker fucked off? There's no more knocking or perhaps I passed out and slept through it. My head swirls as I totter back to check.

The eye has vanished. I ease open the door, with a view to knocking the guy down as any real man would. Bilious light falls on nothing but a tray with the remains of a Room Service meal and a figure walking away, away, right at the end of the corridor towards the lift. On he goes, and on, without seeming to make progress. A hangdog fellow walking the wrong way along a moving floor.

*

'Don't speak to me, just don't. Until I'm fuelled.' Mary's wearing dark glasses. Setting down her tray, she swigs black coffee. 'What was that wine? Brontosaur piss?'

'Cooled a long age in the deep-delvèd earth!' says Jarvis. 'Keats. Forget which ode.'

'By the way,' Mary says, between mouthfuls of toast. 'I've just been embraced. In the foyer of the hall. Pass the sugar, would you, Seb? I need a sugar hit. Yes, your pal embraced me like a sister. On an empty stomach. Oh my Lord. I had this strange sense – I don't think it was the hangover, might have been though – that he's coming apart from himself. Honestly, I kept seeing him double, as if I'd got a lazy eye. Actually I used to have a lazy eye when I was a kid. You know what I mean, Seb? Look.'

Mary makes her left eye swivel out of focus so that she can, she says, see both of me. 'I found this a useful skill when I was a kid. If my parents told me off for bringing dead voles or owl droppings into my bedroom to dissect, I'd just let my eyeball swing out – like – this. See? Kind-of unnerving, right? When they threatened me with an operation, I decided the party trick had outlived its usefulness.'

'Put your eye back, Mary,' says Jarvis. 'You're turning me off my seaweed.'

How can he stomach that mess of laverbread, cockles and plankton, swimming in a liquor of grease? He will be embarking shortly on a new diet, Jarvis announces, which will reveal to the world the svelte man within. *Bara lawr*, he explains, is an essential brainfood. Protein, iron, iodine: you name it, your laverbread has it all.

'But what did Rhys say?' I ask Mary.

'What did he *say*? Don't ask me. And what did he *mean* by what he said? How would I know? Well, let's see – he talked about his daughter – who I assume is real. Apple of his eye. She's a polyglot according to him – translator, cosmopolitan, brilliant, beautiful, et cetera. I take what people say about their kids with several pinches of salt, frankly, especially when they start claiming the kid has good genes on both sides. Anyway, what else? He was talking quite ardently about a woman, forgotten her name. Alice? Eloise? Lisa? Ring any bells?'

Elise, I think. Elise. I say nothing. My mother has never spoken of Rhys, at least as far as I remember.

'This Alice or whatever seems to have been the love of his life but she turned him down flat. Smart lady! Head screwed on. He said his wife – he refers to her as his *second* wife – died. But who was his *first* wife? – the Alice-one who refused him? Oh please. Don't ask! This guy is so deep he has come out of the nether end of himself.'

She finally asked Salvatore why he didn't study something substantial – like a newt or a rat? Anything, really, that was not just a sludge of gloopy metaphors. In any case, Mary told him, she'd heard that postmodernism was passé. And he looked quite stricken: apparently the daughter says the same. He finally said, OK, Mary, if you want wildlife, let's discuss seagulls. They were cruising past the windows with pizza in their beaks. He told Mary about predatory birds he'd seen – the Lammergeier, the bearded vulture, in the Turkish mountains. Like a flying hoover. An angelic vacuum cleaner. Cleans up after us – that substantial enough for you?

Sure, Mary said. Keep with the vultures. And they laughed.

'Well, he's off to his seaside retreat, Seb,' she says. 'He'll be back at the end of the conference, to give the final address. Can't wait. Take that as you wish.'

3

Now, Isis was a wise woman. She was more cunning than
millions of men; she was more clever than millions of gods;
she was more shrewd than millions of akhu-spirits. There
was nothing of which she was ignorant in heaven and earth
… So-and-so born of so-and-so lives, the poison having died,
through the speech of Isis the Great, mistress of the gods.

Egyptian Spell, found at Deir el-Medina[3]

Here at the summit of 'Colomendy', the luxury rest home in
Cardiff Bay, my mother's powers are failing. And she knows
it. Strange though it seems to seek out truth in the temple of
forgetting, this is my one resource. We must speak. Here's the
last vestige of light before the dark. Salvatore's mystical
mumbo-jumbo tells me nothing. It turns my stomach, the
prattle of an inveterate fabulist. One thing is sure: he has
stalked me all my life.

Is it too late to turn to Elise? Even before her current
withdrawals from memory began, for decades we kept
stumm, by mutual consent, about Dad. You might say that
his name perished. Or that together we buried it before it was
dead. Thus the name Jack Messenger unearthed itself by
night, became monstrous and spoke into my dreams. And
never left me in peace.

As we greet one another face to face, an eagle observes me
from a crag in Elise's brain through pale eyes, to me the most
arresting in the world. They communicate an intelligence
both alarming and alarmed.

37

'How are you, darling?'

'I'm fine, Sebastian, why shouldn't I be?'

Colomendy's privacy policy has offered Elise the chance of a self-contained, dignified life, with support. She had a horror of being herded into a television room to play skittles with the addled ancientry. I think she felt her mind crumbling. Flakes fell away in episodes of confusion; caves opened up that she sought to prop – and the props quaked. Intermittently, the light must have guttered. Fear enhanced confusion.

For still the damage remains minor. The great brain keeps its wits about it. It knows how to compensate. Its defensive structure holds.

'Don't you envy me my view?' she asks. 'I'm tempted to watch all day. Cormorants, look. Over there. I chronicle the birds crossing the water. I'm working on my autobiography but the birds will keep making their presence felt.'

The whole outer wall of her suite is glass, giving on to a balcony where Elise can preside wrapped in a shawl, a red beret on her head. From here she keeps watch on the Marina, a plane of ruffled water with remnants of the old docks, the Norwegian Church, yachts and quays. As the weather changes, so does the light, so does mood, so does memory.

Don't put point-blank questions, I remind myself. She'll clam up. As a diplomat Elise's razor mind had been honed and she has lost neither her asperity, cloaked in felt, nor her capacity to close down a conversation. I brew coffee and we start on the chocolates. She shoots me a sharp look.

'No offence but a baby is a parasite,' she says, out of nothing. 'It will leech every particle of nourishment from a mother, even if it kills her. A baby is your enemy, in that limited sense. Isn't that so?'

'Well, I suppose so – in a strictly scientific sense. But—.'

'Now, where were we? Yes, tell me, what are you doing in Wales, dear?' Elise asks.

'Oh, a conference. And I didn't want to lose the chance of seeing you, darling.'

'*Another* conference? Whatever can be left to confer about? So, tell me, how are those mummies and sphinxes and suchlike faring, Seb? Much as before, I imagine. I can't think where you got your passion for cadavers – it certainly wasn't from me. And you have given a learned paper? On?'

I shift in my seat, embarrassed. 'A bit of a whimsical-sounding title – "New Light on the Abomination of Monthu".'

'Dear oh dear!' She chuckles with relish, a luminous silver-grey figure in her immaculate silk blouse, a cameo at the neck. 'Sorry,' she says, choking with giggles like a girl. 'But – honestly! And who or what is or was this Monthu?'

'Well …'

'On second thoughts, don't tell me! What world do you people live in? Wars and invasions and persecution – these, Sebastian, are abominations. Streams of refugees coming out of Syria and Sudan and Iraq – yes, you see, I do keep up with the news and I trust you do too. Sometimes these poor people seem to be flocking out of the TV into my living room. I can hardly breathe for abominations. If you are interested in the real thing.'

I want to cheer her on. She still suffers reality to imprint itself on her conscience. My mother remains courageously enrolled on the side of practical ethics. Elise remains Elise, for all her daunted awareness that her brain may betray her. Snaring her hand in both of mine, I rub it with my thumbs. She must have seen the homage in my face, the gratitude. And, moved by it, she asks if there's anything I need.

'I need to ask you about someone.'

'Yes?'

'A friend of Dad's. Rhys Salvatore.'

'Never heard of him,' Elise says firmly and withdraws her hand. 'Next question.'

I deflate, thinking: whatever did I expect? And my quest seems as anachronistic as a fossil hunt.

I divert Elise by describing a mineshaft I explored in Egypt. My friend and I were checking out Roman mine workings, leaving our equipment at the surface, to try out techniques used by the original amethyst-miners, some of them children. They worked in near-dark, with the most basic of tools. I went first, Aziz puffing along in my wake. We penetrated to the point where the narrowing tunnel fell sheer away. I made out hack-marks on the walls, perhaps left by the children.

I held my lamp over the drop. And there below me was … something terribly human. A basket. Just an ordinary basket of woven reeds like those used by present-day peasants.

'Two thousand years go by,' I tell Elise, who's listening intently, breathing deep. 'Egypt falls. Rome falls. The British Empire falls. The miner's lunch box is still there. Never decaying. Down those shafts nothing changes – there's no humidity. It's not subject to time. The basket remains exactly as the miner left it. Then my friend and I clap eyes on it.'

'What do you suppose they had for lunch, Seb?'

'Bread, certainly. Figs? Fish? Falafel?'

'Couldn't you, I don't know, hook it up or something?'

'I stretched but it was too far down and there was nothing to hold on to. A parlous place to fall – the basket being on a ledge and the shaft pitching way down beyond that. We had nothing we could use to hoist it up. I expect it's still there.'

'And I suppose Aziz was your lover?'

'Pardon?'

'You heard. Yes, of course I know! What kind of ninny do you take me for? Once you asked for a cat,' she continues, without a pause, leaning forward in her chair as if this was the whole point of the conversation. 'Remember that?'

I shake my head.

'Of *course* you can have a cat, your dad said – he was just back from his travels, with bundles of notes to write up and in a sunny mood – and he started play-punching you. Being nice. Of course he was volatile, he could turn. Just like that. In Iran, he told you, every neighbourhood has a *laat*. A boss-cat who beats the crap out of any other cat. We'll get you a *laat*.'

'And what did I say?'

'You said you didn't want a nasty horrible *laat*, you just wanted a pussy cat. To cuddle. Jack started to mimic your manner. As if your gentleness was soft and prissy. As if you were not the offspring he'd envisaged. He was doing these limp-wristed gestures and calling you Pansy. He hurt you; he fully intended to hurt you. I was disgusted. I objected. He said, "Oh but pansies are such tewwibly charming flowers!" I thought: it's something in himself Jack's parodying. You were cut to the quick. But I thought – and this has just come back to me: one day Seb will be taller and stronger than Jack. He's already gaining on him. You see? So,' she asks abruptly, 'when are you going back to Manchester?'

'No, Elise, I'm not at Manchester any more.'

'Oh, I think you are.'

'No, darling. Really. I live in London now.'

'You're sure about that? Think about it.'

*

It was the Manchester of my first love, Justin Knight. And also of James Anderton, Chief Constable and evangelical Christian, who harried gays, accusing AIDS victims of 'swirling in a

41

human cesspool of their own making'. For Anderton queers threatened the straight population. They were rats that harboured fleas that spread the plague. Officers on motorboats cruised the locks and bridges of the Ship Canal with spotlights.

So this is who I am, I thought. Of course I'd always known the nature of my sexuality in a way – but the knowledge had been without substance. I understood not to make undue claims on Justin: they'd scare him off. Amongst Justin's hangers-on, I'd be low in the pecking order. Still and all, I felt … I was going to say, 'happy' – but 'exalted' is nearer to it. Nothing had changed in my world; love had not come, only carnal knowledge. By coincidence, I'd also found a vocation: to become a star scholar like the visiting academic, Rhys Salvatore, scattering light.

Next day police were everywhere and our usual wing of the library was cordoned off. We migrated to Engineering and I sat where I could see Justin, schooling myself to wave and smile only if he did. Which he did. He sauntered past; paused, pushing back a wing of dark blond hair.

'I was wondering, Sebastian – fancy a night out?'

God, yes, I thought, mentally punching the air. I wondered vaguely about the Geek, who had become an accidental arsonist. Weird little sod, I thought. Oddball. Which I somehow, suddenly, wasn't.

Saturday night though started disappointingly, for Justin's invitation wasn't exclusive. The whole world crowded into Justin's room. Candlelight flickered on punkish lads and made-up girls. Although they might not all be girls. Justin had become Justine for the night. I'd expected him to look stunning. What I couldn't have foreseen was that he wouldn't remotely resemble an impersonator.

My lover was – surely, I thought – the real thing, with subtle lipstick and mascara. His fair wig was understated; the blue dress implied rather than advertised the possibility of breasts. We drank, laughed, and everyone kissed Justin and Justin kissed everyone and we all kissed one another. His Tower room, with cartons of stale milk on the windowsill, became a magic, whirling chamber. Later that night we hit a wall of sound and heat and smoke at the Haçienda. Music throbbed through us, noise annihilated thought.

On the street when we spilled out in the early hours I was aware of guys clustering round the beautiful Justin-Justine.

Why wouldn't they?

Through the surging crowd of – were they? yes, definitely – straights, I glimpsed part of my lover's face and his braceleted wrist in motion. First a come-on, then an oh-no, oh please, let me go, don't, I know you're only messing around, and I will give value, but for the love of God don't hurt me.

His head was dragged back and the wig stripped off. I glimpsed Justin's terror.

Huge laughter. Fucking faggot. Poofter. Tranny. Come on, darling, come with us, we'll show you a good time. Guffawing, braying. Fucking freaking disease-riddled arse-cunting whore.

No one went to Justin's aid. I did not. Why did I not? Was it, as I later told myself, that it was all over in one stunning moment? that there were too many people between me and him? or was it that I was crapping myself with fear?

As he was dragged into the car, Justin dropped his golden handbag in the gutter.

*

I wondered if I'd ever sleep again. My mind was all over the place. I'd done a lot of crying in the night and my puffy eyes were half closed. Traffic let loose by the lights at the junction

43

of Platt Lane with Rusholme bellowed past as I made for the infirmary.

The ward sister refused to say how Justin was progressing, since I 'and the literally dozens of friends who keep phoning' were not family. Yes, we might visit, but not in a gang.

I'd never before witnessed the obscenity of violence. Shrinking back, a perfect coward, I'd let the thugs batter my friend senseless. I would always do that, I thought, as I bought anemones at the infirmary kiosk.

Justin had known what was coming, the second the pincer movement closed around him. He'd been manhandled into the car and groped and insulted. He'd been driven to a car park in Droylesden, taken into the bushes, beaten up, stripped and – after Christ knows what other abominations – left for dead.

Justin drifted in and out of sleep. When his parents arrived, we were shooed away and lingered at the ward entrance. His dad, a builder – huge man, as dark as his son was fair – was a complete surprise. Not least perhaps to Justin, who'd complained that his father neither understood nor approved of him.

Well, Mr Knight understood him now. He sat cradling his son's head: 'There's a good lad. Be all right now, angel, you'll see.'

After his discharge, we helped cart Justin's belongings between the Tower and Mr Knight's van. The Infirmary had saved his eyesight; the ruined face was healing. Only after years of plastic surgery would Justin dare show himself again. Even when Harley Street restored his violated face, he was never as he had been. The yobs had trashed some loveliness that was vulnerably innocent. Justin was, he wrote, a self-impersonator.

As I have been. From that day onwards.

'You don't mind if I nod off a little, my sweetheart, do you?'
my mother asks.

Elise, you called me sweetheart. That is enough. Why
should I disturb you by dredging up questions you've had
reason to place out of our reach? I watch over my mother,
extended on the bed, a luminous silver-grey figure, well-
dressed as always, in her immaculate silk blouse, a cameo at
the neck.

I close the sliding door between bedroom and sitting room.
She'll be asleep for an hour perhaps. Time to conduct my
researches.

As a kid I truffled around in Elise's bedside cabinet on
evenings when I could rely upon her absence. She was always
in demand at functions – a dinner at this consulate or that.
My foraging never unearthed much of interest, or at least
nothing I could easily interpret – bar the packet of johnnies
that scalded my fingers. I dropped it with a yelp, slammed
the drawer shut and scarpered.

Now, while my mother sleeps, her hair silvering the pillow,
the pearl buttons on her grey cardigan luminous as the eyes
of nocturnal animals, I am in two minds. Sweetheart, she said,
sweetheart. A woman to whom endearments had never come
easily. For they might prove costly. The territory of the
maternal heart is to Elise (I've always thought) *terra incognita.*
That doesn't mean that she hasn't cared. Unbending as she
is, lacking in comfy qualities, Elise has still been my all in all.
Am I prepared to gatecrash the integrity of her secret world
now that she can less readily defend its frontiers?

Apparently I am. I open her laptop. Guess the password. I'm
in. And rifling through the documents she's been scanning and
the start she's made on her autobiography. It's the business of

five minutes to copy the files to my memory stick: here's a find dislodged from a deep stratum, holding traces of cryptic living tissue. Doubtless this will prove a rather dark form of enlightenment and a grubby form of knowledge. My partner's anguished words come flocking back: 'I've always been second-best – you keep me in the dark – you disrespect me – am I not enough? – why can't you just be straight with me? Even to yourself you are not straight. You range about like a thief in the night.'

*

What is it about Jack? my mother's diary asks in 1979. Light and flighty, wings on his heels, mercurial, he has something coiled within him that is life itself, *life*, she can't think of any other word. Erotic charm is part of it: wherever Jack goes people fall for him, men, women, dogs, cats. It's ridiculous. And exhausting.

When Elise and I arrive home that summer from the Gower cottage, Jack's not in and doesn't appear that night: she thinks nothing of it. Sometimes he'll phone and say, Surprise! I'm in Barbados – or Kenya – or America. That's fine: suits both of them. Elise scans round for a note but there's none. Again, she's unfazed. Eventually she gets round to ringing Jack's friends. No one has seen him.

Odd that he's left the shed door on the latch, swinging open. Elise never goes in there. It's Jack's writing space, just a box but furnished like a tatty palace – wall hangings red and green, with a Persian rug. Two glass tea cups are on the carpet, beside the floor cushions. She sniffs at one – cardamon and rose water. There are sugar cubes on a saucer. So who was with you, Jack? Who didn't finish the bitter chai you brew? Perhaps, Elise thinks, the visitor was uncomfortable with the

Persian way Jack affected, with the sugar cube between his teeth, sucking the tea through it. Terrible for his teeth. And Jack's vain of his looks and scared of the dentist, so he ought to mind. But that's up to him.

The desk is clear of papers – which is unusual. Jack, forever in mid-scribble, generates litter wherever he works.

When she reports her husband missing, police officers have a poke round the shed. Why has she taken so long to report her husband's absence?

Oh, he's often away, she explains, *he has his work, he's a travel writer.*

So – is he a secretive man, would you say? the officer wonders.
Only in the way writers are. A lot goes on under the surface.
So you don't think he tells you everything?
Nobody tells anyone everything.

The shed is ransacked, the carpet rolled up and removed. Colonies of woodlice scatter. Crates of books vanish.

Jack will surface, Elise reassures herself and me. Always has, always will. She rings Rhys and leaves messages. He doesn't get back; is believed to be in Alexandria.

Elise hears me sobbing into my pillow. She doesn't go in to me. She senses the void beneath our feet. Everything rings hollow.

Things move on to another level. The Security Services arrive: public schoolboys with low side partings and pinstripes. – What personal interest does your husband have in the Middle East? What drew him there?

Elise and I are relocated. She remains insanely composed, even when we're told that the floorboards of our house are being raised, the shed disassembled, the garden dug up.

It all comes flooding back as I read the diary fragments and put the bits together. I'd make detours from school on the way to our hotel, passing and repassing our home. I saw masked men in white. A bulldozer. A gazebo, beneath which a body was unearthed. It was that of a boy. I call him a boy because the forensic medics thought him not fully grown, or not quite. He might have been sixteen or seventeen. And he'd been lying there asleep beneath the floor where my father worked, and before the shed was built beneath the turf where I'd done handstands, run in and out of the water sprinkler in summer, thrown snowballs in winter. He'd been there when the garden was a field. He predated the Romans. A root of the beech I climbed had skewered the boy's ribcage and levered him apart. The buried, cloven adolescent had been my constant unseen companion. Once upon a time he had suffered violent trauma to the head.

Nothing to do with us. Obviously. How could he have been?

My mother was questioned about my father. Again and again. I remember moving back into the house and looking out of the window. The devastation wrought by the digger in the back garden began to settle: once the earth had been raked flat, grasses and dandelions rapidly seeded themselves. The garden still looked rumpled as if it had suffered a bad dream.

Together we skinned over the wound we'd been dealt. New tissue formed a film over the festering damage. Elise and I spoke little, each secretive in our own way. Daily I opened the curtains and scouted for Dad, and then just opened the curtains without expectation. After seven years Jack would be declared dead in absentia.

For a while, lovers came and went. I'd thunder up and down the stairs in my boots, to advertise my bolshy presence to whichever stranger had gained access to my home and mother. A parade of academics, diplomats, journalists. Through Elise's half open bedroom door, I'd glimpse her, dressed in too little, bright hair over her shoulders. There'd be glasses of red wine on the bedside table and I might overhear the disputatious voice of an invisible stranger. And the talk that came from her bedroom. Words, words, words. Mandarin talk, lofty and abstruse, sprees of erudition. As if the sex were only foreplay or pretext for this carnival of polemic my mother craved. How ashamed I was of her. What other teenager was disgraced by a mother like mine? If Dad came home, how would he feel to find his bed usurped? I wondered if he'd see what, with dismay, I intuited: that she was more herself for being without him.

In my memory Elise is sitting up with her knees bent, holding her insteps in both hands, rocking slightly, and her bedroom is a debating chamber, a nest of dissent and oratory. She looks young and kindled and intensely vulnerable.

*

When she wakes, Elise says she'll freshen up with a shower. I hear the patter of water and a murmur of, improbably, hymn-singing. She is requesting, or rather requiring, the Great Redeemer to guide her through this barren land. Then she surveys the wondrous Cross. Finally, as the shower is turned off, her variable soprano loudly counsels her soul to be still: words by Katharina von Schlegel to the music of Jan Sibelius.

Silence after these rollicking pieties.

Out Elise pads in dressing gown and slippers, pink and softened-looking like a baby from the bath.

'What I would like you to do,' she tells me, accepting camomile tea, 'is to bring your partner to see me, would you, dear. And you remember that I am composing my autobiography?'

My face burns.

'What's the matter?'

'Nothing.'

'You look remarkably shifty. For goodness sake, let's behave like adults. I will enlighten you under various headings. But be careful what you ask for.'

'Yes, I will bring Jesse. Yes. Thank you.' I half-choke on the words. 'If he'll come. Because we're going through a bad patch. I hope it's only a patch. It's certainly bad. All my fault. Jesse is such a lovely man, Elise, I know you'll take to him.'

'Do you remember,' she asks, 'when you were in the school play, at Radshead? You were, if memory serves, a member of the Chorus of Virgins in *Elektra*. Now, which was it, Aeschylus or Sophocles? There are two plays of that name. Whichever it was, the adolescent lad they cast as Elektra did a lot of caterwauling. You've heard of howler monkeys? His was a very screeching performance.'

'Sophocles, I think,' I said, my heart sinking. We are off on a tour of the Ancient Greeks: I'll be powerless to arrest or divert the flow.

'Of course,' Elise adds, rearranging the cushions behind her back on the couch, and giving the impression of settling in for a nice long literary chat, 'Euripides parodied Aeschylus's *Elektra*, didn't he? Something to do with a fawn. But actually I think this must have been Sophocles after all.'

Go with it, I tell myself, gritting my teeth. In this way we might eventually drift back on to the true path. Or not.

'So anyway,' Elise goes on. 'I'd driven like a demon and been flagged down by the police somewhere in Kent. Now where was it? Broadstairs? I made it just in time to see you in your nice little skirt sashay on to the stage with the other virgins to advise Elektra not to waste her life in mourning. Would it bring her father back? No. And did Elektra take the slightest notice? Of course not. We don't, do we?'

'No, Elise, mostly we don't.'

'We're always walking forward looking backwards, aren't we, Seb? But what I was going to say was: there seemed to be a bunch of mad boys in charge of the lighting. Things would get so dark that you could hardly make out which actor was doing what. And then these delirious light-boys would shoot the dimmers up. The audience was in stitches. It was the most hilarious tragedy I've ever attended. I expect you wonder where all this is going, don't you?' she asks with a look of amusement. 'Well, when I was going through my papers, the mad boys threw up the dimmers.'

'They did?'

'Yes. In my memory. Keep up now, Sebastian.'

'Right. Sorry.'

' Jack's old chum. You were asking about him.'

'But not if it upsets you to talk about it, Elise. Really.'

'No – can't say it upsets me. A long, long time ago. Poor chap, such an empty vessel. Isn't it funny the way these schoolboys don't grow up? They just couldn't let go of each other. Oh, they tried – but when one ran away, the other was haring off after him. Talk about there being three of us in that marriage. And then again they were often at each other's throats. Quite literally.'

'But – Elise – how painful for you.'

'I minded, Sebastian. And I didn't. I had my freedom and space. I've always been self-sufficient – as you know – to your cost, doubtless.' And it's her turn to look shifty and pleading.

'No, Elise. No. You've been –'. I bite my tongue to stop myself trotting out the cliché about good mothers. You couldn't be called a good mother, or even a good enough mother, I think. But you were mine, Elise; and you were there. And you are still here, still mine. And I wonder if she feels the forgiveness flowing in waves from me to her, and the gratitude. I've never called her Mum, let alone Mummy. She has always been her indivisible self. And somehow there are irrational tears in my eyes and I don't know what to do with the arms that long to cwtch her.

'Anyway. Thing is, these two poor little chaps, each the runt of its respective litter, were seven or eight years old, when they were packed off to prep school, to be bullied and abused in the name of civilised British values. Together they located this bolthole. They'd reminisce over it in the most rhapsodic terms. Know what it was? A broom cupboard! A place to escape. Oh the scent of mansion polish and chamois leather! Do you remember when we ...? Etcetera. After that, there was public school and Cambridge – but they never found anything to match whatever it was they'd found in their secret world. So there you are.'

Yes, I see. I think I do. They were far from home. All their lives. Even with me and Elise, Jack was a homeless person. She says nothing about Rhys's proposal of marriage. Perhaps she's forgotten it, if it ever happened.

'So – anyway – about the lights. Rhys was always there in our house, morning, noon and night. Or about to be there. Or being referred to. Oh Rhys this, Rhys that. Jack and he were infatuated with one another but they were also jealous – or envious – rivals. What one had, the other coveted. Once I said to Rhys as we were chopping vegetables in the kitchen (for he was always wanting to enter into household activities), "You can take over from me and be Jack's wife if you fancy it, Rhys, do please feel free – it's quite a demanding job though, I have to warn you." He grinned and said he might pass on that. Said he had something to Jack's purpose nothing. Shakespeare's Sonnets – look it up, Sebastian. But surely you remember Rhys from those days?'

I shake my head.

'He was practically a fixture. He'd take you for walks to the park and the zoo.'

'No,' I object, quite sharply. 'I remember *Dad* taking me to the park. Pushing me on the swing, that kind of thing.'

All Elise replies is, 'Right?' As if to say, Believe that and you'll believe anything.

'He did, Elise. I remember clearly. He did all sorts of things with me. We went fishing. He took me on a steam train.'

'Well, anyway. Don't distress yourself.'

I'm not going to insist or ask further. My mother's raised eyebrows are telling me I've confabulated. Memory has changed the mask on the face of the man who accompanied me on those outings. It's easily done. Apparently.

Rhys at that time was a handsome, quietly charismatic fellow, Elise continues – magnificent head of hair, which he still in the 1970s wore in the hippie-style, eyes pale, with long lashes. Jack had brought back from Thailand for each of them a *pa kao mah*, a sarong, which they liked to lounge around in. Elise was always in jeans and they all liked the feeling of release from constraints of gender. The electricity used to fail: it was rationed, in the time of the strikes and fuel shortages – and, sod's law, usually at dinner time. They'd cook on calor gas and eat by candle light. Those meals would go on for hours. The talk of gods. Except when it was more like the braying of asses. My mother kept a diary, by candle-light.

One evening Jack and Rhys were spaced out, they were dreamy and happy and sloshed. They smoked roll-ups and relived their lives backwards. Finally they arrived at their childhood refuge – in the boarding school cupboard with the mops and the smuggled torch, the place where they imagined themselves heroes and supermen and ate their Homeric feasts of tuck sent by Rhys's mam and thick wedges of bread and jam smuggled from the tea-time meal served before prep and dinner.

The hash was probably helping their mood, and the brandy. The room was brimming with hilarity and that sort of mellow, melting tenderness they felt for each other – and which flowed to include Elise. Perhaps it overflowed too far.

They were discussing courtly love; it was a thing of Rhys's. He was into King Arthur and Guinevere and bold Sir Lancelot, particularly the latter. Marriage is no deterrent to love; jealousy is essential to love; two men may love one woman – that kind of thing. One minute they were in a good place, the next at one another's throats. A candle went flying. It left a scorch mark up the wallpaper, nearly to the ceiling.

Elise remembers a snarl and a rush and the sound of my father's head being slammed against the wall.

Then the electricity came on again: the sobering bathos of artificial light. Jack wasn't moving. Rhys was sobbing over him, saying what have I done?

Elise told him to go and not come back. Ever.

Through his tears Rhys said, softly and quite slyly, 'I did it for you. If you knew what he is, you wouldn't stay with him another minute, Elise darling.'

Then apparently I came downstairs, grumbling and rubbing my eyes. I'd got a chest infection and conjunctivitis and there was a crust over my left eye, which wouldn't open. Elise got a neighbour in to babysit me while she drove Jack to Casualty; he had concussion and stayed in overnight.

'Do you remember any of that, Sebastian?' she asked.

'No. I don't think so.'

'Really? Perhaps you blanked it out?'

'I wouldn't know.'

'Quite. Well, a couple of days later,' says Elise, 'I heard Jack on the phone to – yes, you guessed it. Perhaps they needed the violence. Fed off it. When Jack went missing, I wondered. How could I not wonder?'

'Do you still wonder?'

'Frankly I'm past caring.'

Rhys would have desired any woman Jack had. And so it turned out, she says. Think of it this way: they didn't so much want each other as want to be each other. Oh, it was nothing to do with me: don't think I was flattered, I was just the muddle in the middle. Be straight with people, Elise tells me. Bring Jesse to meet me. Before it's too late.

4

"Yeki-bood, yeki-nabood." That's how all Iranian stories, at least in the oral tradition, have begun, since as long as anyone remembers. "There was one, there wasn't one," as in "There was a person (once upon a time); but on the other hand, no, there was no one."

Hooman Majd[4]

The nearer the train approaches to Jesse, the more I realise, not just that I can share all this with him, but that I need to. It's my only hope. At last, let Jesse in. We've been sharing bed and board in my flat now for many months and yet Jesse has been in some cruel and wanton way locked out.

Whyever does he put up with me? What has he done to deserve me? Jesse practises the decencies, I the indecencies. My truant night walks, how foul they seem today. My mouth fills with queasy sweetness. All this slipperiness can be amended. Jesse is my family, nothing less. I knew that when I asked him for a civil partnership. It flashed upon me that he and I might adopt a child. This thought had sprung, it seemed, from nowhere: I'd never been aware of the least desire for children or been particularly comfortable in their company.

So I asked Jesse. Will you? Dearest, will you? Shall we?

Half an hour after I'd asked and he'd accepted – reluctantly, because he clearly comprehends me better than I understand myself – I'd done an unpardonable about-turn. The night walker had taken my place; the true-hearted lover had melted away.

56

The thought echoes back: 'Don't be like your father, Sebastian.'
What happened to you, Dad? I need to know.

Jack Messenger was shot or had his throat slit on the Turkish border with the Zagros Mountains, frozen into that desolation until the spring thaw revealed his corpse and he began to decompose in the sun. Predators cleaned up the evidence, scattering his remains until a new winter arrested his decay: over and over again. Like so many others he had fled Iran's Revolution and was trying to slip over the border, to find his way to Istanbul. Thence to Alexandria or Malta. But where was Rhys Salvatore while all this was happening?

At Reading, a child's voice says: Daddy?

Men and boys are standing in the aisle, on their way to a match, so I can't immediately place the voice. Here it comes again: Daddy? It's phrased as a query. I turn in my seat: a toddler in scarlet football strip is raising his arms to be picked up, waggling his fingers urgently.

Well, pick him up then. Don't stand there talking goal scores. Pick him *up*.

*

Letting myself in, I lean against the door, thinking: At last, home, peace, groundedness. It's a boundless relief. The Barbican architect built the walls of the apartments thick. You could kill someone in here and not be heard – or die and be forgotten. There are no audible neighbours – and often owners of these affluent pads reside elsewhere for most of the year. All we generally hear is the fizzing of water over the concrete cascade in the lake quadrangle, and the occasional plane.

But there's a subdued turbulence in the flat. My first thought is that some drunk has got in and is shambling about: Scottish, or pretending to be, and declamatory. Silence, then

a burst of laughter, knocking noises. Fuddled, alarmed, I shed my coat and scarf and hang them on the stand. It's as if my key has turned in the lock of the wrong flat.

I peer round the living room door. A figure lurches across the floor, beer bottle raised, spot-lit by a couple of lamps. An audience seated around three sides of the room turns towards me as I enter.

'Faith!' slobbers the alcoholic in a parody of a Glaswegian accent, toppling against me, waving his bottle in my face. 'Here's an equivocator! O, come in, equivocator!'

He performs a sweeping bow. Someone is rapping with his knuckles on the table. Who the hell are these?

'Hey,' says Jesse. 'Seb, hi. Sit down a minute and let the porter finish. I'll explain and introduce you.'

I slump down while the far-gone porter renounces his intention to usher through hell-gate those who've gone the primrose way to the everlasting bonfire. His Scots accent is as fake as they come but he seems genuinely drunk. Reaching the passage about the part played by drink in lechery, he produces a stuffed sock from between his legs and wags it in our faces.

'They're not doing the whole bloody play, are they?' I whisper to Jesse.

'Just a couple of scenes, don't worry. You OK?'

Jesse's friends, an all-male troupe engaged to play in the Barbican Theatre, go on singing for their supper. I can smell it in the oven, one of Jesse's vegetarian casseroles, tender and succulent and herby, except that the appetite of a carnivore is incapable of appeasement from Jesse's cooking. My palate's always craving the something else that is lacking – the animal juices he abhors.

Yes, of course, I did know they were coming – and that Jesse's designing the sets. I don't think I recognise anyone.

Only when Lady Macbeth informs us that she has given suck and knows how tender 'tis to love the babe that milks her, cradling a remembered infant to her breast, do I fix my eyes on the actor – who speaks with such fondness that you can easily believe he once suckled offspring and felt distraught when the time came to wean them.

Twenty-odd years ago we'd all visited Justin at Manchester Royal Infirmary, carrying armfuls of flowers.

*

It's a battle between goldfish and gulls, Justin says, which the gulls are bound to win. And he's spied a heron swallowing a koi carp a foot long. What a gizzard! Elegant bird, mind, fantastic piece of engineering – and gorgeous fish those, like jewels. It's fascinating, Justin says, to see a heron slowly stalk the fish and lower its head – he mimes the motion – and dart its beak to skewer the fish of choice. The speed of it! Apparently birds see everything more slowly than we do. What can you do? he asks. It's nature, after all. It must cost the earth to keep replenishing the pond with fish to feast the birds of the air.

Jesse has gone across to the theatre with the director to work on the play's design and lighting. What we need to say has not, by tacit agreement, been said. Perhaps this evening, after the dress rehearsal – for tomorrow I return to the conference.

'You must have done rather well, Sebastian,' Justin says. 'To own such a pad, I mean. I saw you once on television. Inside some ancient tomb somewhere – setting the world right about jackals. Jackal gods. In the dark. Couldn't see you very well. I was impressed. I thought to myself: well, *he*'s kept all his hair.'

'And you! Very much so.'

'The pony-tail suits you. Yes, I was sorry we lost touch. I'm not a great correspondent,' he says, graciously taking the blame upon himself. 'When I sit down to write a proper letter, I enjoy it. But Facebook has spoilt us for all that.'

Justin and I corresponded for several years and, as I tell him now, I kept all his letters. He has a gift for correspondence, making of small and inconsequent events memorable miniatures that he has elaborated and polished just for you. After the attack, Justin cocooned himself, unvisited, for some time, until his face was ready to emerge. The letter-writing made a kind of mask for him.

The last time I saw Justin was when his parents came for him. He'd not be staying on at Manchester. Well, he might return when he'd fully recovered. When, as he said, he'd been put back together again. But that was unlikely to be for a year or two – and by that time most of us would have moved on. And now, although no traces remain of the complex engineering Justin has undergone, he is not exactly as he had been. But then, who is? Justin doesn't refer to the attack, at least not directly, so I make sure to keep clear of the subject. Unspoken, it looms between us. We make our way through the labyrinth of walkways past the ponds towards the Conservatory to contemplate the terrapins and finches and quails. A wedding is in progress.

'So – I gather you and Jesse are not hitched?' he says. 'Legally civil-partnered?'

'No. Not that we haven't spoken about it. But. Well. What about you?'

'Likewise. Not quite grown up yet, to be honest. Hoping to, of course. One day. Just, not yet, O Lord, not yet.'

'I know the feeling.'

'Yes, I noticed,' he says and laughs. 'You are a wanderer.'

'Oh, thanks very much! I didn't think it showed.' What has Jesse told him – or told them? Or is it just that his nose detects a moral smell coming from me?

'No offence. Takes one to see one, eh, Sebastian? Jesse is a lovely guy though. People think they can mess him about, don't they? They learn differently.'

Still smarting, I don't ask how he knows this. But he tells me anyway. A younger member of the troupe was at primary school with Jesse, who was in charge of the form guinea pig. This guinea pig enjoyed the happiest life of any known rodent. It ate only the best salad, from Jesse's mum's kitchen – and grew plump and sleek. Jesse would communicate with it in a language of whistlings and purrings and swore it was the most intelligent of pets. When he caught someone teasing it, he knocked the kid down. How come I don't know this, about the guinea pig, about people messing quiet Jesse about?

'And what happened to the guinea pig?'

'Nothing. He kept it safe. Well, I suppose it died in the end of old age.'

We come to a standstill. I think: I do not fully know Jesse, although I break bread with him every day. I stare at Justin.

'What?' Justin's hand goes to his cheek in a defensive gesture, as if some fissure might have opened in the armour of his loveliness.

'No. Nothing. Sorry. I was just thinking about … bread. And trust.'

My mother once remarked that they had a phrase in the Middle East: we are bound by bread and salt. I think that was it. This was the one bond you could not betray and that could never fail you. The bond of bread and salt forms the bedrock of reciprocal human relationships, on which all trust rests. Forfeit that, and all is lost. I say none of this and yet it seems that Justin hears it, or the gist of it.

61

'Trust is something I learned that day, Sebastian,' he says, breaking the silence. 'Oddly enough. The violence of the world and its hate: how you can't rely on the world from moment to moment to stay peaceful – and yet you have to, don't you? Otherwise you couldn't go on. And the kindness of strangers. Not quite an antidote.'

*

'My dear,' said Jesse fondly. It's the old Jesse, temperate, forgiving: the attentive person with the gift for listening, both to what is said and to what's withheld. But then he says, 'If I'm honest, I don't know what's to be gained by talking.'

I try to tell him about my stalker. And about Elise. How she invites him to come and see her.

Jesse's having none of it. 'I'm not sure if I can any more, Seb. I feel – just – drained. I can't tell you how tired I feel. All I want to do is sleep.'

The sleeves of Jesse's cream pullover are rolled up. He sits beside me on the edge of the bed, bent double, elbows propped on his knees. He doesn't look at me. I lay my palm on the inside of his arm, where the pale veins fork, and stroke the intimate skin. It comforts me to touch him. He removes his arm and shakes the sleeve back down as if my touch had riled him. He shivers. With a great yawn, he ruffles his hair with both hands.

There's nothing conspicuously attractive about Jesse – except everything. Bread and salt, I think. And the mad idea sweeps over me – not for the first time – that if I could have had someone's baby, it would have been Jesse's, and all would be well. Or if he could have had mine. The biological absurdity of this idea doesn't really strike me. I've felt it before, fleetingly, as we lay in a loose hug half asleep at the end of a tired day.

'Jesse, I'm so sorry,' I say.

'You always are, I do believe you when you say so, I really do. But it's pointless. Don't start. Not now.'

'What do you mean, don't start?'

'Look, sorry, I'm just – really tired. I've never been so tired in my life. I need to sleep. And don't wake me up in the night, for God's sake.'

'Jesse.'

'I mean it, Sebastian!' he bursts out. 'I've had enough of all that. Enough.'

I swallow hard. Flush to the roots of my hair. My voice comes out small. 'All what?'

'All the stuff we pretend not to know about, we pretend isn't happening. It used to hurt me. Appal me. I used to think it was my fault. It's beginning to bore me.'

'You don't sound like you,' I mumble. What I don't add is that he actually sounds rather like me. Taking hold of the reins at last, resisting, controlling. I've never thought how much that unique ability to listen, the exceptional empathy of the man, might have cost Jesse. And how much temptation it has offered me, not only to take him for granted, but to trample all over him.

Without reply, Jesse lies back, turns on his side and falls fast asleep, just as he is, fully clothed. When I ease off his shoes, he hardly stirs. I inch in beside him. It's the first time in our life together that I don't dare reach out to him. Has something happened while I was away to put iron in Jesse's soul? But what? Is there someone else?

Sleep doesn't come. I lie in the lee of Jesse's breathing. It comes like sea-waves, in a hushed rhythm, steady and remote. A respiring tranquillity, over there, in which I long to take shelter.

In the early hours I give up on sleep and stand at the

63

bedroom window, lifting a slat in the blind to peer out: there's what they used to call a bomber's moon. In the milky brightness, I can make out St Giles Cripplegate, where Foxe and Frobisher and Milton are sleeping. The pond holds the moon quite still. What is all this fuss I've been making about the past, when it comes to it? Even my father is old history, stale and unsustaining. Rhys Salvatore is nothing to me. Only my mother and Jesse have any call upon my heart. The lumber of my obsessions is tomb furniture: viscera preserved in a canopic jar. I have allowed my parents' world a mortuary persistence.

When I turn from the window, Jesse is awake.

'Off on one of your jaunts?' he asks. 'Don't let me hinder you.'

'No,' I say. 'No, of course not.' I perch on his side of the bed. My ulterior mind dives to the questions: how does he know, how long has he known and what precisely does he know? Or think he knows. 'I'm going nowhere, Jesse. Can't sleep. I thought I might smoke a joint.'

'OK.'

'Have your sleep out, love,' I say. 'Sorry to wake you. We can talk in the morning.'

'No, it's all right. I'm used to it.'

I make hot chocolate and root out some ginger biscuits. Jesse rolls the joint, puffs and holds, passing it across between finger and thumb. Perhaps hash will soften his sardonic turn of mind. I've bruised him so badly. I've made a habit of reaching in and roughly handling Jesse's heart. Why? Because I could. Not once but countless times. Now his grief, so long constrained, is in process of turning rancorous – and anger will free him. Justin's words echo: 'People think they can mess him about.' A clear warning.

'Jesse, could I say something? I know it solves nothing. But

I do – just – love you.' I'm hardly able to look him in the face. 'As I have never loved anyone before. In my life. Please, please – dear, darling Jesse – would you at least believe that? – if you believe nothing else.'

He takes another drag, clasping it deep in his lungs and blowing out a thin stream of smoke. I feel him falter. Then he tells me.

The night before I left for Wales he heard me get up and dress, as he'd done before. He watched through his eyelashes as I picked up my trainers and tiptoed to the door. It wasn't new. Always before, he'd let it happen. He'd exercised restraint and given me the benefit of the doubt. As soon as I closed the front door, he threw on a tracksuit and followed.

'I can still hardly believe, Sebs, I can't – that you'd behave like that. To me. To yourself. Even though I half knew. But half knowing isn't the same as seeing with your own eyes. As I followed you, you seemed like another animal. You looked smaller. You even walked differently.'

My palms sweat. I'll stop. On my honour it will never happen again.

He makes no effort to disguise his cynicism. Honour? I'd have felt just the same in Jesse's position. Any person of average intelligence would sneer at the clichés I find myself coming out with. I swig back my chocolate. He hasn't touched his. I stop myself asking him if he'd like a biscuit. I go blurting on. I've no idea why I behaved like that. Well, I do have some idea, but there's no excuse for it, none in the world. So I won't try to explain. It is, in some horrible way, mechanical.

Yes, Jesse says, he knows that: mechanical. When we were first together, he thought I was sleep-walking. In fact there were occasions in the past when I had sleepwalked. He'd shepherded me back to bed.

'What was I doing?'

65

'One time you tried to clamber into the mirror. I did my best not to wake you up, just guided you back to bed. You'd do things that were not really in character. Weird. You cleaned the bath with bleach. Another time you made toast and spread it with Marmite, which you normally dislike.'

'You never said, Jesse.'

'No. I didn't like to. I felt it might disturb you.' Jesse's voice is softened.

'Actually,' I venture, cupping my hand around the weak flame of intimacy. 'I used to love Marmite when I was a kid.'

'Fuck the Marmite, Sebs. Fuck it, fuck the childhood memories. I'm not interested. You reek of nostalgia, did you know that? I'm assuming you admit to being awake when you go off cruising?'

'I'm awake. Yes, of course I am. Jesus, Jesse —'

'No, Sebs, I'm not Jesus, you see. I'm plain Jesse, with feet of common clay. I value decency. But all the rest of me is clayey too. Perhaps that's your mistake.'

He assumes I was bare-backing, he adds. Bringing back shit knows what infections. Bringing death into our bed.

No, I say, oh no, never – it was only ever –

'Only ever fucking what?'

'You know.'

'But that's it, I don't know.'

The shame of having to declare it. The frantic relief of rushing to offer Jesse honest reassurance. I haven't risked his health or his life, never would. He flushes, his lip quivers – reassured? No. I can hear him thinking, You kissed me with that mouth.

The joint has burnt down nearly to its tip: I motion him to finish it. He lies back against the cushions and the dressing gown falls open across his chest. Jesse gazes at me impartially as if trying to put his finger on what species of insect I am. A

forensic stare. Drawing on the joint, he spits the ember into a saucer just in time.

'So. Is there someone else, Jesse?'

'How can you even ask that? What world do you live in, Sebs? You don't know me, you don't know me at all, do you?'

In bed Jesse turns his back; then somehow, still high, we're fucking. It feels wrong — it feels right — it hurts like hell – it gratifies – it's an act of erotic vengeance, accepted in a spirit of remorse. Foul. Some force in my brain seethes and fizzes like a bulb that's telling you it's about to blow, it's been going downhill for some time, and now it's on the point of …

When he drags himself off my back, slick skin sucks against skin and comes away with a cartoonish smacking sound. Shaking and bathed in cold sweat, I manoeuvre myself round in the bed, a heavy, yeastless dough of flesh. I flop down beside Jesse on the rucked sheets. Always afterwards we'd kiss, sliding asleep in one another's arms. He has taught me this tender language of belonging. Now Jesse's back is turned and we fail to kiss. Which feels – it's an odd word – profane. The perishing bulb splutters a biblical phrase: *If thy right eye offend thee, pluck it out.* Shivering convulsively, I edge on to my side, dragging up the duvet and placing one palm on Jesse's back. *Pluck it out and cast it from thee, pluck it out.* Through the slats in the blinds, strips of dull daylight leak, rippling over the back of Jesse's head and bare shoulder. I nuzzle his neck with my forehead and cup his head in my hand. *If thy right hand offend thee, cut it off and cast it from thee.*

I remember a phrase I'd heard someone use in the dark past. Not to me. 'If I fail you, take my eyes.' Whoever said it covered both his eyes with his fingertips and I felt in that moment the pulsing jelly of my own eyes nestled beneath unsafe lids. One poke of a finger has the power to blind. It's a monstrous forfeit to offer for a broken vow.

Later, brushing my teeth, I hear Jesse showering. Through the frosted glass I see that he's lathering his belly and groin repeatedly, as if he feels defiled. He'll be in the theatre all day, he's said, working on the set. With his friends.

'By the way,' he adds as he pads past me, a towel round his waist. 'I forgot to give you this letter.'

'I need to tell you, Jesse. Everything. Unreservedly. At least, everything I know. Not as an excuse – but as something I owe you. If you'll hear me, darling, hear me out?'

'Yeah. OK. But don't call me darling. It makes me itch.'

*

The inscription on the envelope reads: Ava Salvatore – Translation Services – Arabic, Chinese, Farsi, Turkish.

Ah, the stalker's daughter. Just what I needed! Chip off the old block? Ye gods, how many more Salvatores are going to come creeping out of the woodwork? Isn't one of you more than enough? Sitting in the cafe at Paddington Station, near the sushi circling on its conveyor belt, I break the seal with my thumb, though I'm hardly interested. It's Jesse who fills my mind's horizons and imprints himself on every thought.

Salvatore's daughter writes briefly that she feels I should see the enclosed, which has just come to light. There is doubtless more, she says. She gives an address in Bristol and a phone number: I may get in touch if I wish. The enclosed is a scanned copy: the original, which of course I'm welcome to see, is not much clearer; in fact she would say that, counter-intuitively, it is less clear.

When I open the enclosure, yes, I'm interested.

Minute scrawl spiders down both sides of the sheet and, finding its path blocked, creeps into corners, then doubles back on itself, as the writer turns the page upside-down to

write from bottom to top; the writing crams the margins, until scarcely a morsel of blank remains. He's writing in pencil – and I know which pencil – and his paper supply has apparently run out.

I smell something that cannot possibly be present: Turkish cigarette smoke. At home in Fulham, rays of compromised sunlight penetrated the blue-black swirl of toxins that passed for air in our living room: you saw how choked we were with Dad's smoke. From his lungs into my own poured the rank breath of my childhood. He smoked above my crib. They both did. Ash fell on my pillow. Perhaps I shall die of it.

The smell clung to his jacket, tweedy and bristly against my childish face. Dad! Daddy! What have you brought me? I'd leap up into his arms. The memory of this is so violent that it eclipses all thought of Jesse. Come home, I think, come back. There'd be some keepsake for me in his pocket, a fossil, a pebble, a pumice stone – something unique and precious. My boy eternal! Dad said, hunkering down to my level, cupping my face in both hands to inspect it before whirling me in the air.

I smell the smoke and see the propelling pencil in his jacket pocket alongside a matching tortoise-shell fountain pen – the tools of his trade, to which Dad's fingers would stray, to check that he was armed. This is my gun, he said. The long, fragile leads were kept in a tobacco tin, in a bulging lower pocket. These are my bullets. Woe betide a child who touched the forbidden tin.

Where's the mouth and where the tail of this letter? It's written in fragments, illegibly dated. I'll start here, with what looks like *Azizam*. Beloved. The endearment he used with my mother. How Salvatore's daughter got hold of a letter to Elise I cannot imagine. I take a run at the whole screed before attempting to decode in detail.

Jack cajoles. He's just *Azizam*'s 'hopeless shambling old Neddy the Donkey, led by the nose through the world by curiosity, hee-hawing all the way.' Can his darling ever forgive him? Jack promises: never again. He tried to resist the wanderlust but obviously not hard enough, for here he sits, in yet another tight spot, awaiting transport. He asks *Azizam* to kiss their little one for him.

Escaping the Ayatollah's Revolution, Jack has hitched his wagon to an Iranian grandee with a plump wallet and a network of contacts. 'Keep this letter safely – I'll need to use it for *THE* Persian book, *azizam*.' This book he confidently expects will make Jack Messenger one of the greats of all time. Walter Thesiger, Martha Gellhorn, Patrick Leigh Fermor, eat your hearts out. And of course this letter is meant as copy. Life for my father was worthless unless written about.

Ex-official of the National Iranian Oil Company, Mirza's swinish activities under the Shah hardly bear thinking of: no wonder the guy needs to disappear. As Jack waits in Mirza's opulent apartment (his servants will strip it of valuables when they leave, that's their cut) the oilman bemoans his vanishing privilege. Bred in a harem, Mirza insists that the eight wives all got on a treat – and their sixty-odd offspring ditto. Those were the days, Mirza says. Our women were happy then.

Dad's Great Book will be entitled *Man in a Burqa*. He'll be travelling as Mirza's wife. Don't worry, Mirza reassures him, nobody will violate your modesty. Jack finds this piquant. Visibly invisible, he'll be a roaming eye. His Better Half hands over to the people-traffickers an eye-watering wad of cash, receiving in return false passports and detailed instructions. Keep your eyes down, Wife. No talking. Walk small. Mince. Like this. That's the way. And hide your hands and wrists. Mirza, even in this emergency, chortles at Dad's pantomime

aptitude for his camped-up role. Happily, as an old pen-pusher, Dad's hands are rather feminine.

Hubby explains that the traffickers will not receive full payment until they're safely in the West. He trusts the Kurdish loathing of the Turks, the Arabs, the Shah and the Ayatollah. You can rely on hatred. Hatred is sound. Hatred is glue.

The cars arrive. In the burqa there's a torrid microclimate and you breathe your own fiery carbon dioxide. A black-framed grid limits your view. Peripheral vision: nil. The thick fabric gusts in and out. It smells in here of fusty, ageless female misery. Jack trots through the airport in his master's wake, as a wife must. A short-arse like him comes into his own. Nobody looks at Jack, for the simple reason that he is nobody.

Once you're on the plane, the Kurds have advised, fall asleep instantly, OK? Wake up as you're landing. Dad's wedged in a row of shrouded females. All nod off as soon as heads touch seats. What if they're all males in drag? No way to find out.

They taxi, lift off, bank; leave Teheran behind.

As they land in Rezaiyeh, Hubby does not turn to acknowledge Wifey, who scuttles humbly in his wake. A Kurdish car takes them to the Turkish border. Up, up and up. At a shack on the mountain-side, a ravaged woman in rags – no teeth – wearing a turban – comes out carrying Russian automatic submachine-guns.

Jack's given a rifle; hides it in his burqa. I can feel him enjoying every moment, flying high. He has disappeared into his disguise and feels crazily safe. There's snow in the hills, only a light dusting so far. They pass through a kind of – what can he call it? Arms fair! Never in his life has Jack seen such a gallimaufry of guns – antiques from British colonial days,

71

Soviet stuff, old Nazi gear. Hubby's Kurds, traders themselves, pause to hail others but then, with night approaching, they press on.

I make out that they've reached a Kurdish Village, close to the Turkish border. Grubby barefoot kids; two haggard wives; soiled mattresses; upwards of forty guns leaning against the walls, museum-pieces. Hubby, used to fine dining, turns up his nose at the rice and meat they're served; Jack hoovers up every scrap, coaxing his Other Half to eat. More snow is expected and they may have to hang around for weeks. As Hubby shivers, Jack sheds his burqa and is thrilled by cold and freedom.

Three of Hubby's brothers have been relieved of fingernails and genitals before being executed. Hubby weeps and Jack tries to offer comfort. 'It's strange, *azizam*, you start to care for one another. Intimately.' Hubby blows his nose and, pulling himself together, graciously enquires after Jack's family, his children; does he have sons?

'Am choked, can't reply at first. I say: I have a daughter.'

Both men are bathed in tears. Hubby asks her name and age. Jack goes all to mush and it's Mirza's turn to comfort Jack.

What? I must be misreading. Jack is asked – Have you a son? And my father replies that he has a daughter.

My father is writing a letter to – Christ, I don't know any more. I've no fucking idea. I'm confused, I must have misread. I look up and the station rocks with a thunder of wings. There's a bird, a trapped pigeon.

It definitely says daughter, I have a daughter.

Who are you writing to, Jack? This cannot be Elise. There's a knife in my chest. I feel the blade there, a raw pain in the trachea. I breathe shallow; my fingertips probe the burning bone. Thirty years ago Jack Messenger on the Iranian-Turkish

72

border plunged a blade in his boy-child's chest and left it there.

No sons. Only a daughter.

Mirza takes Jack's hand and squeezes. And Jack is moved, it's the strangest moment. The two of them burrow down under the cover together and share body-warmth. Jack dreams appalling dreams.

Azizam is so young, he laments. He has lived a motley life. Is ashamed. He needs to unlock his heart about secrets he should have shared with her long ago. With *azizam* he can at last be wholly himself. Her heart-melting eyes. Her grace of being. He found her late in life and she accepted him with all his blemishes.

'I was – am – mortally afraid to lose you.'

As he scribbles, there on the mountain, fag drooping from the corner of his mouth, there's something this constitutional liar finds himself wanting to confess to his … whatever she is … *azizam*.

How much did this youngster know about him? I notice that he stops short of confessing anything significant. If he can get home from the Zagros Mountains, confession may never be exacted. He prudently keeps his secret – a wife his own age, a son – to himself. Because after all, there's no chance that his lying can actually be expiated. He'd be required to choose and perhaps neither spouse would fancy living with such a lowlife.

So off he goes again. He's near the border now.

Get up, get up, come on! Now! Jack's been dead asleep. He thinks it's Prep School all over again and he's slept through the bell. Oh shit, a caning offence. Where is Rhys? Rhys, where are you? Not safe, not safe. Jack scrambles into consciousness and finds himself, again, in extremity.

Burqa on. For a quarter of an hour they drive through snow

and dark. – Get out, run, come on, hurry. Jack drags portly Hubby, hauls him, gets behind and shunts him along.

The Turkish frontier post. The Kurds can be seen through the window of the guard post drinking, smoking and horsing about. Hubby and Jack wait silently. They don't look at one another. Dawn breaks: a weird snow-light and salmon clouds in the east.

Their Kurd appears, demanding a substantial bribe for the Turkish guard. An impossible sum. Hubby's magician's hand, vanishing into an inner pocket, emerges with the cash. Their Kurd will take yet another cut of this bonus, that's understood..

And they're free to cross.

If – no: when – they reach Istanbul, Jack will post this letter home and the woman known as *azizam* and her daughter can start expecting his return.

*

When I phone, Ava Salvatore assures me that, yes, sure, this is a perfectly good time. As good as any other. She's been up all night but there you are, she says. She sounds businesslike, rather formidable, faintly irked by my stammerings. I see her as a starched sort of person, hair scraped back, in a dark suit. The echoes in the station forecourt pulse and the trapped pigeon has alighted to take advantage of the remains of a bagel amongst the polystyrene.

Ava Salvatore explains that her stepfather has sent her, by Special Delivery, a packet of documents, including his will. She and I are named as joint heirs and co-executors. She thought best to get in touch at once.

'Rhys is your stepfather? He always talks about you as his own daughter.'

74

'Yes. He would. He's a terrible plagiarist. Stolen property is his hobby.'

'But your father … and my father …'

'Yes.'

'So you are my – ?'

'Half sister, I gather. May I ask: what did you know about us?'

I'm staring up at the Departures notices, in company with a horde of stressed-out passengers. We're all frowning upwards for light. A train will move, but when, and from which platform, is not revealed. Everything has come to a standstill. Copper wiring, the tannoy announces, has been stolen from the track between Paddington and Reading.

'What did I know about you? Nothing,' I say. 'I knew nothing whatever about you. Did you know – about us?'

'Only for four days.'

'Ah. Where did your family live?'

She reveals her childhood address. I reveal mine. We both gasp. Our father took as his lover a girl not out of her teens. A man with a wife his own age and a son, he relished concealments and told himself: what they don't know can't hurt them. O come in, equivocator. And it seems he installed a second little brood a quarter of an hour's walk from our house in Fulham, for ease of access. And when he died, his friend, having been turned down by my mother, stepped into the breach with the second family.

Ava has no memory of her natural father. She has only ever known Rhys. Her mother was twenty-one when Jack disappeared; twenty-four when she married Rhys; not quite thirty when she died of cancer.

'I'm so sorry.' My feet begin to shuffle me away from the departures board, to stand in the lee of a florist's where no one is buying flowers. Passengers whisk past. A woman

comes out, wearing a chador, and plunges an armful of lilies in a bucket. She wonders if she can help me and I shake my head.

'Let us waste no tears on ancient history,' says Ava brusquely.

Where do we go from here? 'Do you have any idea why your stepfather sent you the documents at this point?'

'He wants us to make contact? I don't know. I see him very little nowadays. You're at this conference with him, I think, Sebastian?'

It's the first time Ava has spoken my name. I explain that I took some time out and I'm just going back for the last day – seeing my mother en route.

'Your mother? She's …?' She hazards the question tentatively, and in a voice so soft I have to ask her to repeat the question.

'Elise is, yes, alive – and well – if rather frail. At least, in one sense she's frail. In other ways, the most powerful character I know.'

Our father, in his arrogance, assumed he could hold his two broods apart forever. Did he think himself not only invincible but invisible, slipping between adjacent worlds? Well, he did get away with it, didn't he? He was invisible. He is invisible. Meanwhile Rhys Salvatore watched and waited, hungry for any leavings his idol left unconsumed.

'How much did your mother know?' I ask.

'Mummy didn't tell me things she thought would hurt me. If you decide to speak to your mother about all this, Sebastian, greet her from me – if that seems the right thing. But if you feel that would make her unhappy – it's bound to really, isn't it? – say nothing.'

'Thank you, Ava. And we'll meet? You and I?'

'I think we should. Oh dear. Hang on just a minute.'

There's a siren or car alarm going off. Or – no – someone is crying. The wail gains in volume and pitch. Ava's back at the phone and explaining that it's her baby, Luca. 'He's teething or something and didn't exactly sleep last night.'

I could not have guessed. A sort-of nephew. A hint of a future. The voice of my sort-of sister has altered tone and timbre and a blessed ordinariness enters into our exchange. She has morphed in my mind. I see Ava now as a woman in posset-stained pyjamas, hair all over the place, holding things together, just about.

'Dieter, will you take Luca? Dieter! Thanks. Give him some Calpol? What time did we give the last dose? – Just a minute, Sebastian. – Can you take him, Dieter? – OK, my partner will sort Luca out while we finish. When you come down to it,' Ava says, quite matter-of-factly, 'our father was not just a bigamist – he seems to have been a bit of a sex tourist. There was apparently *another* relationship in Egypt, Sebastian, another family. There are letters in Arabic. Did you know that?'

*

I'll ask her. Straight out. What did you know, Elise? What do you remember? How did it affect you? No, of course I won't. That would be sheer brutality. I need to absorb this. Meet Ava. Talk it through with Jesse.

Elise has something to ask or tell me, that's clear. She's like an athlete on her marks, an impression reinforced by her hoodie and trainers and the impatient jiggling of one knee. Meanwhile I may as well take the chance to calm down from the intense emotion. Fetching deep breaths, I carry tea out on to the veranda. The city lies greyly amorphous under low cloud, swallows casting brief reflections on the unruffled water.

'When did I ever ask you for anything, Sebastian? Seriously, when?'

'Well – never really, Elise. But you can ask me for things, of course you can. For anything.'

'I don't know about *that*. Mrs Nextdoor has got her daughter in a stranglehold. A head-lock. I overheard her telling someone that your son is your son till he gets him a wife but your daughter's your daughter for the rest of your life. And really, I did quail for the daughter when I overheard that. It's a bleak lookout to have to wait for your life until the ancientry kicks the bucket. Although I have to say that Daughter seems a jolly soul and not to mind. I suppose the jollity's part of the role. Her name is Milly.'

'So – you don't wish you'd had a daughter?'

'No, dear, I've *been* a daughter, and that is plenty. If I had *had* one, you can be sure I would not have named her Milly. Milksop kind of name, like Milly Molly Mandy. Sebastian, you are your own person. That's enough for me. Whether I was ever enough for you – is another matter.'

I reach over to adjust Elise's cardigan round her shoulders and, with a wincing shrug, she extricates us. 'Well, enough of that. And I'm not cold. I'm not a bodiless head, you know!' she tells me, incomprehensibly.

'Well – no. But –'.

'Frankly, dear, I've a yen to swim. Not in a chlorinated pool with ninnies trolling up and down in lanes. Real swimming, Sebastian. In the sea. I'm thirsty for it! You can wear your underpants when you come in – what colour are they? – navy, fine, nobody will mind or even look.'

The sea at Rotherslade's still as a millpond – a mercurial shade of grey, and the tide well on its way in. Elise is fine on the steps but the high bank of pebbles leading down to the soft sand is slightly hair-raising. How strange: she's lost a good inch

78

in height. But she's fit and so far has suffered no falls with their attendant breakages. I hold tight to her hand. One can imagine the fragile bones snapping – and, if they did, she'd never be the same. It would mark the beginning of her downfall. The thought of taking Elise into the icy sea fills me with trepidation.

She sits in a folding chair, silent, hands clasped in her lap, and seems pleased with everything, from the drifts of fishy-smelling weed to the headland's dark green flank. In the old days she was a prodigious swimmer.

'You know Dora came here to die?' she says. 'My old Marxist pal. Surely you remember Dora? She drowned herself. Just by those rocks over there. I was so happy for her. I did a little jig when I heard.'

'*Happy* for her? You did a *jig*?' My worst suspicions are confirmed.

'It was a good way to go, Sebastian.'

'I hope you aren't thinking of following in her wake. Because, if so, I'm marching you straight back to –'

'Relax. Dora was ill. She chose a better way. It was a rational choice. Anyway, down to business.'

The sun has broken through a film of cloud and the sea glows like pearl. Elise fits on a pair of prescription goggles. Optician's free offer with reading specs. What do I think?

'You look the business. The real deal.'

'Are those your manpants? Don't worry, nobody's looking.'

Hand in hand my mother and I pick our way through the muddle of pebbles and shells towards the sea. Gentle waves lisp in and break softly at our feet; there's almost no surf.

As I cringe and cower, Elise takes off. I watch her freestyle out, an efficient glide, paddling herself forward. Where Dora died, Elise lives.

Afterwards I swathe her in sweaters, towel her feet and hair. Your son's actually your son for the rest of your life, I

think. Yours, my darling, will never get him a wife, after all. Or a husband, come to that. I pour tea from the thermos and ask if her thirst is quenched now. She thinks it is, for the time being. Don't fuss, she silently admonishes me: for this is life, the fullest life, and we have to live it now. Somewhere inside myself, as I minister to her, I feel that my heart is breaking. Elise has learned to live within the passing moment but I stand nakedly open to losing her. The secret of Ava has retired to the perimeter of my mind.

'What I fancy,' Elise says, 'is chips from the cafe.'

'Fish with them?'

'All right then, why not? Yes, and afterwards, ice cream. Find out what flavours they have. Debrief the girl exhaustively. You don't need to come back to tell me – if there's chocolate, that's my first choice, especially with pecans – then mint, not strawberry, though strawberry is better than nothing. Don't come back with nothing. And coffee – Americano, not cappuccino if we're having chocolate ice cream. But otherwise – fine. Oh, could you also get a bar of chocolate – hazelnut – in case we get peckish later?'

'Anything else?'

She gives it some thought. 'Not for the present.'

Although it turns out that Elise can't finish the chips, she makes a remarkably good fist of it, and lapses back, patting her belly, saying that this is the life and why don't we look into purchasing a beach hut?

'I have something important to show you at home,' she says. 'An item of attire. It will change our lives!'

She has never been remotely interested in how she looks. I give up.

On the way back to Colomendy, she says, squeezing my hand, 'Funny to think that last year I'd have been glad enough of a visit from the Old Man's Friend.'

'How do you mean? The Old Man's Friend?'

'Pneumonia. Carries you off with no fuss. A nice little dose of pneumonia once seemed all I could reasonably hope for. To cease upon the midnight with no pain.'

'I'm sorry you felt like that, Elise, when you first came here. You should have said. Or I should have known.'

'Anyway. Sorry to hear about Jesse,' she says. 'Never mind, dear. Friendship is the great thing. Think of George Herbert – how does it go? – *And now in age I bud again.* But you have to seize the moment. To get budding. The Ancient Romans knew that, Catullus and so forth.'

My head swims. Catullus met the Old Man's Friend a very long time ago.

'I've lost interest in my autobiography, I'm afraid. I've stuck all the junk in the green recycling bag.'

Elise looks sleepy when we arrive back at Colomendy. But also exultant. With a flourish, she opens the wardrobe door to disclose what looks like a hanged man. It's a wetsuit. She brings it out proudly and shows me the extras: a rash vest, a strange little helmet, rubber gloves and bootees. The suit looks impossibly heavy and cumbersome. And that's where I come in, apparently. To help her in and out of it.

'So we can keep going all year round,' Elise explains.

5

*STREPSIADES: Vortex? Well, that's something I didn't
know. So Zeus is now no more, and Vortex rules instead of
him …*
PHEIDIPPIDES: Who says that?
*STREPSIADES: Socrates of Melos and Chaerephon – they
know about fleas' footprints.*

Aristophanes[5]

There were partners before Jesse, some closer than others,
none bonded to me as kin. They came and went, leaving little
trace. I remember the ritual of stripping the bed the moment
they'd gone, bundling sheets into the washing machine, with
their rank spoor of random sex.

One morning I opened my eyes to see a blond guy
prowling my bedroom. Blondie had silently dressed and was
lifting my wallet delicately from my jacket pocket. He
fingered out maybe two thirds of the notes. Every so often he
checked that I was still asleep. I studied him through my
lashes. The guy's attention swivelled to the shelf of Egyptian
deities. He weighed them in his palm, like a connoisseur. A
silver replica of Anubis. Real silver? Any value? You could
almost hear the ticking of his pea brain. Blondie hadn't
seemed to take to the jackal god. His fingers hovered over
several miniature ankhs, in rather the way my mother
ponders the choice of chocolates. Unexpectedly, Blondie
returned to snatch Anubis. Into his pocket he slipped the god
of death.

The guy's flaxen hair stood on end like a corn stook and he appeared, in the shaft of daylight, all of sixteen, though he must have been twice that age. His skin wasn't good, acne-pitted from adolescence. He had the decency or prudence to leave my cards intact. I observed him curiously, fascinated by his experienced frisking of my belongings. Blondie was tough – clearly used to regular workouts at the gym – but I felt safe in challenging him. As I grabbed his wrist, he capitulated with a foolish simper. I turned out his pockets and took everything, including Blondie's own wallet, which I emptied. Ron, was that his name? Rod? Something with R? Or not with R at all? Just – basically – no one. The guy was prey and I let him go. And the odd thing was, I felt rather exhilarated than otherwise by the encounter.

Shall I return to this barren cycle of predation when Jesse leaves? Perhaps I'm an addict and should check in to some clinic. There has been a relentless thrill in my night walks, in the anticipation rather than the outcome, slamming into some anonymous body, without consequence. Losing Jesse, the bed will be barren, food hand-to-mouth. I'll ride the circle line of conferences and speaking engagements. I'll teach my graduates and peer into each fresh face for something that has escaped me.

Don't be like your father, Seb. Find another way. He called the girl *Azizam*. There was a daughter. Another family in Egypt? Really? And? Who else? What if there are others too, like the spawn of sperm-donors who've fathered a thousand children? It's laughable. I don't want to know.

Salvatore's concluding talk is eagerly awaited, though not by Mary, who welcomes me back to the conference like a sceptical friend of many years' standing. Or rather, an inseparable friend of her scepticism. She also took a break, she tells me, spending a day in Pembrokeshire to seek out

ancestors – but, hey, she fell in love instead. With the hedgerows and the heathland and the sea. I nodded off, Mary says, on a bed of thyme and red fescue. You can sometimes feel the earth's slow heartbeat beneath you, and then you wake, and there's no time. None at all. Just this moment. Your bony hip rests on the calcite of limestone. As we amble back to the campus, she's describing the puffin colony and flocks of sanderlings haring hilariously along the tide line. It's a joy, it's a privilege, Mary says, to view such life and to have our moment and know that we are related. Close kin to birds and fishes, our surname ought to be *Euphanerops:* the first fish with fins at its butt-end. Legs-to-be that propelled us out of the slime.

We wander down towards the khaki beach, wind tossing strands of hair across her mouth, grit lodging in the bud of my eye. Is this autumn that's approaching in the seethe of leaves as we mount the wooded incline towards the bay? A remnant of last year's copper beech leaves still adheres to the mother tree, archaic deaths challenging for space with new deaths.

I could tell Mary everything. And perhaps I shall. Just not now. Until I've got everything I can out of Rhys. And meanwhile, I'll enjoy her company. In her plaid shirt, frayed jeans and cowboy boots, Mary looks more than ever like a country and western singer. Any minute she'll burst into song: *OK, so you're a rocket scientist? – That don't impress me much!* I tell her this; she laughs and, taking my arm, asks after my mother. The more she hears about Elise, the more impressed Mary is. Why don't we travel back to London together tomorrow, and stop off in Cardiff to say hi to Mom? And I'm not to forget that there's an ever-open invitation to Montana: a dinosaur with my name on it is waiting in a cave.

Mary's skinny jeans are in rags: distressed and destroyed,

she explains – these being technical terms. She does it herself with a razor, the trick being to avoid ripping the under-layer of white cotton. No need to go for designer distress and destruction when you can make the mess yourself. I laugh aloud. Tell me something I don't know. We wander the tide-line, past the dunes with their charred remains of cold fires. The salt-pickled log where I sat that first day – I can see it, further out now, and Salvatore's has been washed away by the tides. We end up at the Lido where hardy children are splashing about on the verge of winter. Mothers huddle at the edge, hugging themselves.

Over coffee I ask about Rhys: has Mary seen anything of him? It seems he's retired to his Gower cottage, like Horace to the Sabine farm, to recreate himself in preparation for his lecture. For oddly enough, considering his charismatic reputation, Mary has heard that he suffers from performance nerves. He anguishes in advance over every word of a public lecture, racked with self-doubt. But when the dreaded hour arrives, he'll soar up in an afflatus, abandoning the script to extemporise.

I plan to do a citizen's arrest on Rhys, is how I phrase it to myself. Face-to-face I'll put the questions I've feared; tell him about the conversation with Ava; ask about Dad. The questions will be answered, or not answered, and laid to rest. I've texted Jesse to explain I'll be home tomorrow with much to tell him. Locating kin? I have it already. I pledge myself to work at finding a remedy for the breach between us.

The closing lecture is a celebrity event. Salvatore's name has worked its magic, for numbers are swollen with students taking advantage of free entrance. Mary, Jarvis and I slide into the back row of the packed theatre, to hear a talk entitled 'Hauntology: The Third Lobe'. The students seem to be part of a fan club. A young woman with green hair informs Mary

that, once, Rhys spoke for six hours, breaking for lunch on the dot and resuming in mid-sentence – and that *everyone came back*. It was in Paris. They honour ideas there, they dare to think – Rhys is an original, a dying breed.

'You – are – kidding,' says Mary. 'Aren't you?'

'No, really.' The green girl's eyes behind her fashionably owlish specs are quite round. 'He's a legend? You know? My friend was there. Said it was, like, apocalyptic? Intellectually?'

I am mesmerised by the green hair. It seems to segue into a sheen of purple.

Mary says, 'My god, the old windbag. Let me out.'

'Give it a go though,' the girl urges.

'No way. I don't have time to throw away.'

'Honestly though. Stay. You'll be mesmerised. Do you like jazz?'

'Well, yes,' Mary says. 'But what's that got to do with it?'

'Rhys's speaking is, like, a riff? – a Charlie Parker solo? You know? Just as you think it's ending, off it goes again?'

The guy next to her cranes round. 'Rhys has a quarrel with Death,' he says. 'Endless procrastination, endless deferral. And you need to hear him out, you're part of the music, right? Takes you up with him beyond where your mind can go, it's true.'

The aisles are crammed, in defiance of Health and Safety. No escape. Fug of carbon dioxide. I'm feeling awry. Shit. Green hair. Quarrel with death. Family in Egypt. The Messenger tribe. I have a daughter. Third Lobe.

'What's the Third Lobe exactly?' I ask the fan club. They've no idea but the thought excites them.

In the antechamber just beyond the swing door I spot Salvatore hovering, havering. The very tall Chairperson bends to him; seems to be coaxing, caressively, her hand on Salvatore's sleeve. Thinking of running away, are you? That

would make for a nice short lecture. But now he's at the lectern, in a dark suit without a tie. His forehead gleams with sweat. His mouth opens. We wait. He waits.

'I live my death in writing,' Salvatore informs us breathily, as an opener. 'I posthume as I breathe. But I digress!'

And everyone laughs, roars, claps. At least, the *cognoscenti* do. As if he were a pop star recalling past hits. Why the laughter and applause? No idea. Mary has no idea. She mimes garrotting herself.

'It was Monsieur Derrida, I think, who coined the term *hauntology*, in mockery of the philosophers' penchant for *ontology*,' explains Salvatore. And we learn that hauntology is to do with … smartphones. We're invited to get ours out. A forest of phones waves in the air. Mary types an email into hers. Jarvis offers us a winegum. We learn that smartphones discourage commitment to the here-and-now, fostering a ghostly Presence-Absence. The web has brought about a crisis of over-availability that, in effect, signifies the loss of Loss itself: nothing dies any more. Everything returns on YouTube or as a box set retrospective.

'Ah, this grave loss of loss! Could anything be more harrowing?'

Salvatore looks round at us as if awaiting sorrowful confirmation or correction on this point. And – the way he's standing – looking round the room, throws me further off-kilter. There's a tremendous wobble of time. I recall, as if it were all passing before my eyes, that strange crossing of paths in Manchester. For the more Salvatore denies our haunting by ghosts, the more mine come swarming. Justin crosses the concourse, holding himself with conscious grace, with his dark blond hair and his loveliness, beautiful and mortal. The Geek with his acolyte in the library stacks repeats Goethe's deathbed plea: *Mehr Licht!* and is answered by a sudden beam

87

of torchlight. The scholar with the Che Guevara look who has come in search of a son stands in the foyer beside the spectral printing press, with its screw like an instrument of torture.

'What's up, Seb?' whispers Mary. She nudges in to my shoulder.

'Nothing. Migrainey feeling. Ignore. It will pass.'

Yes, that's all it is. The old trouble. The mind-melt. Nothing to be done. I let the deranging light shock my right eye. It will pass. Everything will pass. The lecturer is still lecturing. On and on. It's what they do. Wind them up and they go off for an hour until the battery wears out.

He's saying something about Aristophanes. *Fleas' footprints.* He can't really have said that.

I'm falling. Into the mindmelt. Nothing for it but to sink my head on to my hands. Some door in my head opens with a pang. Someone steps through.

Is he coming for me? Am I dying then, I ask myself. Who will care for Elise? Who will tell Jesse how dearly I loved him and bless him for the road? Nothing to be done. Occasionally, I think, Jack took time away from being Jack to be just your dad. You woke up howling and in he came, still warm from sleep, tying the cord of his blue and white pyjamas. Lifting you up.

'Are you not well, Seb?' Mary whispers. 'Seb!'

'I'm OK.' I wince.

'We'll escape when we can,' she says and lays her hand on my shoulder.

Shush.

Where was I? Yes. He holds you but the nightmare remains below, waiting in the troubled sheets of your single bed. So you cling on hard and cry, he shows no impatience but accepts your fear, for hasn't he known fear and loneliness? He murmurs things to you, of strange lands he has visited,

and the Inuit throat singing of Ungava Bay that goes like this … ha ha! yes it does! – and the Tibet Om Music that goes like this … yes darling, isn't it lovely and soothing – and you drift off, knowing … this was real. Occasionally.

'Let me quote from Nietzsche,' says the big noise at the lectern.

'Oh, please don't,' murmurs Mary. 'Spare us. Seb, you are worrying me, let's go.'

What is clear is … this. Truth occurs in moments. Only. Sandwiched between the lies and duplicities. These moments, they make no difference. They are void of consequence. Having happened, they can neither be confirmed nor – please note – undone.

'Seb, let's go. You look awful.'

'Aura. It's passing.' I raise my head and squint. There's the old fraud, quoting Nietzsche who was himself quoting Montaigne who was quoting Aristotle, for there is nothing new under the sun. And what Nietzsche said was, *O my friends, there is no friend!*

'I wanted to tell you a story about a friend who died. For him I nourished a contrarian adoration. But when the Third Lobe kicks in – my friends, loss is lost; the abyss sinks into the abyss. End of story! The mother of all tumours is growing in my brain. The thing is so big now it's a third lobe, an organ of thought.'

He pauses and passes his hand over the right side of his skull. A huge gasp from the audience. Rhys grins and shrugs, and says with cynical detachment, 'Where was I? No idea. Anyone tell me? Of course you can't. Oh the terminal tedium of the academic merry-go-round. Frankly I think I'm dying of boredom.'

He gathers his papers together, shakes them, switches off the lectern light and departs. I let him go. It's unimportant.

There are just the moments. Hang on to this thought. But what was it? I let Mary lead me out like a blind man.

*

'Don't cry now, Sebs,' Jesse says gently.

'I'm not crying.'

'You are. What a shock for you – the terminal illness of an old friend.'

'It's not that.'

'Come on now, love,' Jesse says. 'You can't be blubbing on the train. We can talk, of course we can. You can tell me everything. There's plenty of time. Sebs, are you there? Listen, we'll always be friends.'

My train comes in and we end the call. I've left Mary with Elise at Colomendy, explaining there is something I absolutely need to do, which can't wait.

The train loses pace; crawls to a halt; backtracks. No voice explains. Someone cracks open a beer can.

'Oh God, my connection!' says a woman. 'What about my connection? – I'm supposed to be in Lübeck first thing tomorrow morning.'

I close my eyes. There's no hurry. I'm going nowhere. With Jesse I should have learned better. Our Lübeck idyll returns poignantly. We were just friends. I recall the train journey from Hamburg Hauptbahnhof between forests of silver birch; crossing the River Trave and drawing into the glowing ochre of the medieval city. All kindled by intimations of the unsaid, as we made our way to that peculiar labyrinth where we were to lose ourselves and find one another.

In hot sunshine we walk past the Holstentor, locating our hotel on a quiet side-road: small, clean, serviceable. We have brought along a travel kettle and brew up tea in Jesse's room. How

90

moving it is to visit the fallen bells in the Marienkirche. In the Thomas Mann Museum, we spot a youth who's a dead ringer for Mann's enrapturing Tadzio in *Death in Venice*, even down to the sailor-suit. The child looks into our eyes, one by one, with an angel's unfaltering gaze, and turns away. Afterwards we wander in the muddling miscellany of dwarf passages, remains of the mediaeval Lübeck, where the poor lived crammed on top of one another, for the city, constrained between rivers, could only expand upwards. Squeezing our way along, we enter an intricate maze, each *Gasse* darker than the last, and chillingly cold – for no sun reaches in except, briefly, at midday. The narrow dwellings are now elite pads, with tiny courtyards. It's like being trapped in a pleasurably sinister fairytale.

Squeezed breast to breast between cold walls, Jesse and I pause to kiss. Nothing has been spoilt; it is the pristine morning of our time together. Which is, irrevocably, over.

*

Ava's translation of Hafez slides from my briefcase. There's a tipping point, her Introduction tells me, when absence becomes presence. The mind can only wait and abide and be open. This is the only way.

When have I ever waited and abided and been open?

Leafing through the poems, I think that Hafez's ghazals have passed through my half-sister's mind, diffused through her consciousness like the wine they sing of. Ava has spent her adult life brooding on the gap between languages, seeking correspondence between two closed and ambivalent systems. To live in the company of Hafez is to appreciate the slippage between words, between worlds. The poet's meanings are profoundly equivocal. Or rather: profound in their ambivalence. Erotic ecstasies are also images of mystical love.

91

They are both, they are neither, they are untranslatable under any system. It follows that whichever language Ava inhabits at a given moment is haunted by the ghost of the other.

Iranians have a tradition of using Hafez's *Divan* for divination, Ava writes. Try it! Ponder your heart, my reader, and silently put your question. The first words your eye alights on will be Hafez's mystical message to you.

Why not? I close my eyes and consider formulating a question. What should it be? What exactly happened to Dad? Is that too coarse a question for Hafez to answer? Probably. The thing to do would be to put a question in a language that acknowledges Hafez's own. It should be a question about love, or wine, or roses, something capable of resonance within the murmuring body of the lyrics. Like a note that arouses a musical instrument.

I hold the book between my palms and search inwardly for my question. When it comes, it surprises me. The question is tender and just. And it has issued from deep inside me, the temple where my love for Jesse took up residence over a year ago.

I ask my question aloud. 'How can I best love Jesse now?'

Beloved, you are dawn, I the candle in the night.
Smile, and I burn away my soul's last light.

The couplet resonates across seven centuries and thousands of miles, travelling across the gulf between languages and, as it flies, morphing, until it becomes an echo of an echo of its original. One loves, but the condition and cost of one's love is personal annihilation.

To be himself, Jesse must outlive me. Yes, I think, I see that, my darling, I do see it. Hafez has answered. It is strangely comforting.

[1] Homer, *The Odyssey*, Book II ('The Kingdom of the Dead'), 520-4; 528-9, as translated by Robert Fagles (Bath: The Bath Press, 1996).

[2] Demosthenes, *Speeches of Æschines against Ctesiphon and Demosthenes on the Crown*, as translated by Henry Owgan (Dublin: William B. Kelley, 1852), p. 92.

[3] Egyptian spell reproduced in A. G. McDowell, *Village Life in Ancient Egypt: Laundry Lists and Love Songs* (Oxford: Oxford University Press, 1991), pp. 118-20.

[4] Hooman Majd, *The Ayatollah Begs to Differ: The Paradox of Modern Iran* (New York: Random House, 2008), p. 1.

[5] Aristophanes, *Clouds*, 423BC, as translated by Ian Johnston, (Arlington, Virginia: Richer Resources Publications, 2008). 380; 830.

ACKNOWLEDGMENTS

I am grateful to Parvin Loloi: all quotations from Hafez are taken from the translation from the Persian by Parvin Loloi and William Oxley, *Poems from the Divan of Hafez* (Brisham: Acumen, 2013).

Any mistakes of interpretation, or liberties taken with verisimilitude, are entirely the author's responsibility.

I am grateful to my agent, Euan Thorneycroft of A.M. Heath, for all his support, and to Richard Davies and Robert Harries of Parthian, for their exemplary work on the manuscript.

I record here my debt to the late Nigel Jenkins, in gratitude for many luminous conversations about shorter fiction and poetry. I thank my friends and colleagues at Swansea University, Anne Lauppe-Dunbar, Francesca Rhydderch, Alan Bilton, David Britton, Fflur Dafydd, Liz Herbert McAvoy, M. Wynn Thomas, Glyn Pursglove and Neil Reeve, for their help, humour and encouragement. Thank you to Andrew Howdle for decades of conversation about Greek mythology and literature; to Julie Bertagna, Rosalie Wilkins, Helen Williams, Rob and Sue Leek, Stevie Krayer and Frances Hill for their constant support. My loving thanks, as ever and for every reason, to my children, Emily Davies, Grace Foster and Robin Brooks-Davies.